"Just tell me you wanted to be with me," Matt said as they walked into the front yard.

"I did want to be with you," Natalie admitted huskily.

Matt pushed her gently against the huge trunk of an elm tree and kissed her. The unexpected touch made her lips part with a low moan.

"Nattie," he breathed against her cheek. "When I kiss you, I want to know that it will always be my right. I want to know that even years from now I'll still be able to reach out and touch you—love you."

Her breath caught with shock. "Matt—I—you don't know what you're saying."

He pulled back just a few inches and cupped her face in the palms of his hands. "I *do* know what I'm saying." He looked deeply into her eyes, and Natalie was aware of nothing but the sharp beating of her heart, the feel of his rough skin against her face, the warm taste of his mouth still lingering on her lips....

Dear Reader:

The spirit of the Silhouette Romance Homecoming Celebration lives on as each month we bring you six books by continuing stars!

And we have a galaxy of stars planned for 1988. In the coming months, we're publishing romances by many of your favorite authors such as Annette Broadrick, Sondra Stanford and Brittany Young. And that's not all—during the summer, Diana Palmer presents her most engaging heroes and heroines in a trilogy that will be sure to capture your heart!

Your response to these authors and other authors of Silhouette Romances has served as a touchstone for us, and we're pleased to bring you more books with Silhouette's distinctive medley of charm, wit and—above all—romance.

I hope you enjoy this book and the many stories to come. Come home to romance—for always!

Sincerely,

Tara Hughes
Senior Editor
Silhouette Books

STELLA BAGWELL

The New Kid in Town

Silhouette *Romance*

Published by Silhouette Books New York

America's Publisher of Contemporary Romance

To my son, Jason,
and our summers of
little league baseball

SILHOUETTE BOOKS
300 E. 42nd St., New York, N.Y. 10017

Copyright © 1988 by Stella Bagwell

ISBN: 0-373-08587-7

First Silhouette Books printing July 1988

Printed in the U.S.A.

STELLA BAGWELL

is a small-town girl and an incurable romantic—a combination she feels enhances her writing. When she isn't at her typewriter, she enjoys reading, listening to music, sketching pencil drawings and sewing her own clothes. Most of all she enjoys exploring the outdoors with her husband and young son.

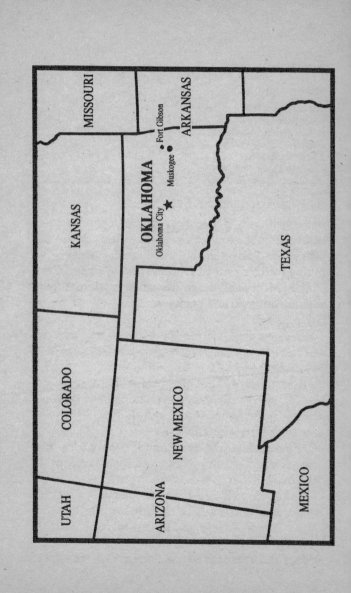

Chapter One

Natalie Fuller shifted her position on the hard plastic seat and recrossed her legs for what seemed like the two-dozenth time.

The school cafeteria was filled with parents and other adults who were generous enough to donate their time for the summer baseball and softball leagues.

At the front of the room, behind the makeshift podium, Leonard Tully was taking advantage of the crowd, playing on their consciences and their pocketbooks to make this year a successful one.

The merest hint of a smile curved Natalie's lips as she tucked a strand of dark auburn hair behind her ear and listened to Leonard's enthusiastic speech.

"And folks, let me add this one, final note: we're not just talking about money here. These kids need our time. When it comes to them, our time is more precious than money. If we don't have anyone willing to give up some evenings and weekends to coach these kids, we might as well throw in the towel. We won't need the uniforms, the batting helmets, the balls or anything else.''

Just like every other year, there was an uneasy rumbling in the crowd at this particular point in Leonard's speech. The same eight or ten people would volunteer to help, too, while the rest went home thankful there were at least that many who were crazy enough to tackle a bunch of eight- to fourteen-year-olds.

''As to the fund drive for uniforms, we've set the pancake breakfast for the second Sunday in April. I believe we'll get a better showing on Sunday since everyone will already have gotten dressed and gone out to church that morning....''

As Leonard went on with a few details about the pancake breakfast, Natalie let her eyes wander. Most of the faces in the crowd were repeats from past years.

Four years ago, Natalie had volunteered to coach when her son, Bryon, had been old enough to play tee ball, which was like baseball, but the ball was hit off of a tee, rather than being pitched. Now that he was a tall, lanky eleven-year-old and had moved up to the faster-paced older league, she was still volunteering. But Natalie didn't do it out of guilt or obligation to Bryon. She loved working with the kids, seeing them have a good time, seeing their athletic skills develop, teaching them good sportsmanship and how to work with others.

True, it was hectic at times. There were at least fifteen players on each team. And corralling fifteen rowdy, energetic boys wasn't easy. But all in all, it was a fun time for Natalie, and each summer she looked forward to the challenge. She only hoped that this time she'd be teamed up with someone other than Dan Jenkins.

With a slight turn of her head, Natalie could see him. Dan and his wife, Rachel, were sitting just to her left and one row back.

Dan's face had that let-me-at-'em look about it. As Natalie tried to hide a grimace, Rachel caught her gaze and gave her a quick, warm smile.

Natalie forced herself to return the smile, but as she turned toward the front of the room, her smile quickly faded. Dan Jenkins was a middle-aged, dedicated family man with two sons and a long career on the Muskogee fire department. He knew a lot about baseball, but none of that mattered when he got out on the field. He was like Jekyll and Hyde. As soon as he set foot on the diamond, he changed into a gung-ho monster. He pushed his son to the breaking point and bullied the other boys almost as badly. The game was all perfection to him—perfection and winning. But that wasn't what the program was about at all, not to Natalie.

Dan had been her partner last year. Surely Leonard wouldn't put her through the frustration of another year with him. In fact, when the meeting ended, Natalie decided, she'd corner Leonard and make sure he didn't. But who would be her partner then, she wondered. Bob Maynard's large, slightly obese figure loomed two rows in front of her. Well, she thought with an inward sigh, Bob didn't know much about the fundamentals of baseball, but he was great with kids. His jokes and antics kept them laughing. That was better than Dan's obsessive, no-nonsense attitude.

Maybe some new man or woman would volunteer this year, she thought with hope. But she wouldn't hold her breath waiting for that one. There weren't any new faces in the crowd that she could see. And the women who volunteered preferred to work with the girls' softball teams.

Natalie scanned the crowd again as Leonard answered a few final questions about the pancake breakfast. There were about fifty or sixty people present, but Natalie knew them all. She'd lived in Fort Gibson, Oklahoma, for the past thirteen years. Here were the same old steadfast, dependable folks that the community always counted on when a helping hand was needed. No chance of having a new coach this year, she concluded.

"That's it, folks. If you have any questions or problems give me a call at home any time after five. The kids are looking forward to a good season, so let's try to make sure they get it. Thanks for coming tonight and we'll see ya at the games!"

Conversation hummed and chairs scraped against the tile floor as people began to get up. Natalie stood, brushed the wrinkles from her white culotte and turned to grab the handbag she'd left on the seat to her right.

As she straightened, she found herself looking directly into a stranger's face. He must have been sitting in the chair right behind her—that was why Natalie had failed to see him earlier.

"Evening, ma'am," he murmured, touching his forefinger to the brim of his gray cowboy hat.

"Good evening," she said with a polite smile. He was young—in his twenties, she'd wager. His skin was tanned to a deep brown, in vivid contrast to the light blue shirt he was wearing. His eyes were almost the same color as the shirt. At that moment she found their clear color very intriguing.

Natalie averted her eyes, feeling a bit embarrassed. She didn't look at men that way, and anyway, Leonard was on his way out the door. She wanted to head him off before he left the building.

Stuffing her clutch purse beneath her arm, she moved along with the people in front of her as they filed through the makeshift aisle of cafeteria chairs.

Before she could reach the double doors, the cowboy's lean frame suddenly appeared in front of her. Surprise was written all over Natalie's face as he turned and deliberately blocked her path.

"Whoa," he said with an engaging grin that seemed like it was only for her. "What's your hurry?"

Well, she could hardly tell this stranger why she was rushing to catch Leonard. Just the fact that this man had even spoken to her was shaking her usually calm exterior. She said the first thing that entered her mind. "The meeting's over."

The corners of his mouth tilted in amusement. "Yes, I realize that."

Natalie drew in a deep breath and struggled to gather her wits. Who was this man, anyway? Why had he chosen to strike up a conversation with her, of all people? Her eyes locked with the sapphire blue of his, and her pulse danced an erratic little jig.

"When something is over, that usually means it's time to go home," she said, then blushed when it dawned on her how inane that sounded.

The half-grin on his mouth deepened. "I know. But I'm new around here. I thought I might find out more about the program before I went home."

She wondered where his home was, then chided herself for wanting to ask him. It should hardly matter to her where the man lived. "Then you've got the wrong person. Leonard is the one who can answer all your questions."

The man wanted to tell this shy, attractive woman that Leonard didn't look the way she did, but good manners stopped him. She didn't appear to be the flirting type at all. In fact, the cool, distant messages she was sending made him think it had probably been a mistake to stop her in the first place.

"Well," he said with a shrug, "I guess you're probably not involved with the baseball end of this anyway."

Her brows lifted at his statement and he chuckled at her haughty expression. "I mean, because you're a woman and all."

She knew he was teasing. Somehow that upset her even more. She wasn't used to being teased by a man, and certainly not by one as attractive as this man was. She looked around, noticing with a sense of panic that nearly everyone had filed out of the room.

Trying to ignore how warm and husky his laughter sounded, she asked, "Do you think women don't know anything about baseball?"

Natalie watched, fascinated, as a faint blush crept across his good-looking face. "Guess I never really thought about it," he drawled. "None of the women I've been around knew much about it."

She frowned, wondering what kind of women he'd "been around." "Maybe you've never associated with the right ones," she offered. Then, deciding she had to get away from this man, she sidestepped him before he could stop her.

To her dismay, he caught up to her with light, quick steps just as she reached the building's concrete portico. At this distance from the street lamps, the light was not very bright. Yet it was strong enough. Natalie could see humor still creasing the man's tanned features.

She had to admit his looks and his avid attentions to her were more than disturbing. She turned away from him to desperately search the parking lot for Leonard.

"You may be right about the women I've known," he said with another husky chuckle. "By the way, what's your—"

"Excuse me," Natalie interrupted, quickly stepping out from the darkness under the portico and into the reassuring beams of the street lamps. "I've got to catch someone before he leaves."

She was gone before the man could say anything else. He watched her hurry across the parking lot toward Leonard Tully.

Well, it was just as well he hadn't gotten her name, he thought. She was probably married, anyway, he thought with disappointment as he stepped off the sidewalk. His boots crunched their way across the gravel parking lot. The next time he saw her, if he ever did again, the husband would probably be along.

Natalie was relieved to see that someone had stopped Leonard before he climbed into his car. She went through the motions of unlocking her car while waiting for the conversation to end.

From the corner of her eye she watched the cowboy cross the far end of the parking lot. His tall, lean frame moved with a graceful ease, and she wondered again who he was and why he was here. He didn't look the type to have a child signed up for one of the teams. No, that one was definitely bachelor material. No wife, no child, no strings—the kind of man she avoided. What business would he have here? It was more than likely that he'd been contracted to do the renovation on one of the baseball diamonds. That was the only logical reason she could think of for his being at the meeting. However, try as she might, Natalie did not understand why he'd singled her out. Fort Gibson was a small town, but it wasn't lacking in available females.

Her face burned at another idea. Might he have taken her for one of those?

The stranger climbed into a black Ford pickup and pulled into the street. Natalie jerked her eyes away from the truck's retreating taillights and back to Leonard. It wasn't like her to be distracted by a man of any sort. It surprised and irritated her to realize she'd given this one a second look.

The man who had been speaking with Leonard finally began to walk away and Natalie took the opportunity to head Leonard off before he slid behind the steering wheel.

"Hey, do you have a minute?" she called.

His broad face split into a grin. "Anything for you, Natalie. You're one of my best coaches."

She smiled faintly at Leonard's bit of flattery. "Well, I hope that carries a bit of weight. I wanted to ask you a favor."

"Oh, yeah? What is it?"

Natalie took a deep breath. "It's about Dan Jenkins. I don't want to offend anyone, but please, whatever you do, don't pair me up with him again this summer."

Leonard's brow lifted in surprise. "Oh, I didn't know you and Jenkins had problems last year."

Natalie felt a blush creep across her cheeks. "We didn't have problems, not really. Dan is a nice man—until he gets out on the field."

"I know he gets carried away at times—"

"It's more than that, Leonard. I don't like his rigid attitude, so if it wouldn't be too much trouble, do you think you could line me up with someone else?"

He patted her shoulder reassuringly. "No problem, Natalie. And don't forget. Friday is the first practice for the boys' teams. Will you be ready?"

Natalie nodded with a relieved smile. "Sure, Leonard."

The drive back to her house was a short one. In a matter of three minutes Natalie was pulling her car into the driveway. A porch light burned, illuminating the steps that led up to the front door.

Natalie pulled the car to a stop in front of the two-car garage. The split level house of red brick had been her home for twelve years. Soon after she and James had married, James had decided they should invest in a house and property. They'd lived there together for five years. Then James had been taken from her in a shocking, violent way. On his way to an emergency at the hospital, his car slid on the icy highway and slammed into a diesel rig.

There was no pain now when she remembered James, but she supposed the house would never seem the same without him.

As Natalie stepped into the living room she saw Bryon stretched out on the couch, his attention riveted on the TV set. On the opposite side of the room, her mother-in-law sat crocheting a brightly colored afghan.

"Hi, Mom," Bryon said. "How'd the meeting go?"

"Fine," she said, tossing her purse onto a rolltop desk. "Looks like you're going to get new uniforms this year." Natalie turned to grin at her son.

There was very little about Bryon that resembled her. He was tall and thin, whereas Natalie was petite with a figure that would get out of hand if she didn't count her calories. Bryon's eyes were deep brown, like his father's, while Natalie's were a soft, pale green. Her skin tended to freckle along her arms and the bridge of her nose in the summer, but Bryon always turned a deep, nut brown. Natalie's shoulder-length hair was a rich auburn. Her son's was dark brown. Still, there were the same dimples in his cheeks that showed when Natalie smiled, and the same square cut to his jaw that she saw in the mirror every morning.

"That's great!" Bryon exclaimed, scrambling to a sitting position. "When will we get them?"

"By the time the games start," she assured him, then looked across the room at her mother-in-law. "Did you try the cake I left on the bar, Louise?"

Louise Fuller nodded. "A bit heavy for my taste, but Bryon ate three pieces. I tried to tell him all that ginger and cinnamon would give him indigestion."

In the past, Louise's sometimes blunt remarks would have hurt Natalie's feelings, but now she was able to overlook them. Louise was one of those people who tended to find fault with nearly everything.

She and her husband, Harvey, lived in the house next door. Natalie had long ago accepted that the sole reason James chose this house was to be close to his parents. She hadn't blamed him for that, but many times she'd resented it. Marriage was meant for two people, not four, Natalie believed. But James had wanted his parents to share everything in their lives. Natalie could still remember her outrage when she found out James had told his parents he wanted to have a child, long before he'd brought up the subject with her.

But all that no longer mattered. James was gone, and had been for eight years. Still, Natalie sometimes wished she lived somewhere else—a place where she and Bryon could make a separate life for themselves. It was hard for Bryon to come to terms with James's death when the Fullers still brought up the name of their son nearly every day. But every time Natalie thought of moving, she would feel a pang of guilt and resist the urge. James had been the Fullers' only child, and they had doted on him. Bryon was his child, their only grandchild. They'd be crushed if they couldn't see him often.

"Would you like some coffee, Louise? I think I'll have a cup before I get ready for bed."

Louise set her crocheting aside. "If it's decaffeinated. Otherwise I'll keep Harvey up all night with my tossing."

Natalie headed for the kitchen and Louise followed. In the background the television emitted the sounds of squealing tires and gunfire. Bryon would be engrossed until the final credits rolled.

"Well, I guess you plan on coaching again this year," Louise said as she took a chair at the kitchen bar. "That's what Bryon said."

Natalie nodded as she poured cold water into the coffee maker. She knew Louise hated the idea that her daughter-in-law took part in a rough-and-tumble sport, especially one that was so strongly associated with the male sex. "Yes, I'll be coaching this year," Natalie said.

"I know it's none of my business, but have you ever stopped to think that it might embarrass Bryon to have his mother coach his team?"

Natalie's mouth fell open before she could put on a smile she hoped didn't look too false. "Bryon likes having me coach him. If he didn't, all he'd have to do is ask to be put on another team."

"Well," Louise said huffily, "maybe I shouldn't say this, but I'll be glad when Bryon grows out of this summer-league stuff. Then you can go back to spending summers like all the other women do."

Natalie silently counted to ten as she spooned coffee grounds into the basket. "What do you mean, Louise? I didn't know there was a certain way for women to spend their summers."

Louise fidgeted with the tight gray curls framing her face. "You know what I mean, Natalie. In a more feminine way."

Natalie cut herself a piece of the spicy apple cake and served it onto a plate. "Well, I appreciate your concern, but some things have changed over the years. I assure you that teaching a bunch of young boys how to play ball is considered perfectly acceptable in this day and age."

Louise drummed her fingers against the countertop. "Still, I don't think James would have liked it. He always thought women—"

"James isn't here now, Louise." Natalie sighed.

Seeing she wasn't getting anywhere with Natalie, Louise glanced at her watch. "It's getting late. I think I'll say good-night to Bryon and head on over to the house."

Natalie set her plate on the countertop and looked at her mother-in-law. She knew she'd made Louise angry, but that was nothing new. They were very different and now that Natalie was thirty-three years old she was determined to be her own person. She'd lived in the shadow of James and his parents for years. But slowly, step by tiny step, she was doing things her way for a change. In spite of Louise's anger, it felt good.

"There's no need for you to run. It's still thirty minutes until Bryon's bedtime."

"Yes, I know," Louise said, rising to her feet. "But Harvey probably needs me."

"Well, thank you for watching Bryon while I went to the meeting."

"I love being with Bryon. You know that." Louise brushed her lips against Natalie's cheek and left the kitchen.

Natalie let out a sigh of relief and dug into the cake. Moments later she heard Louise telling her grandson good-night, then the click of the front door.

When she was halfway through the cake, Bryon appeared in the kitchen. He went straight to the refrigerator and pulled out a gallon container of milk.

"Who's going to be the other coach, Mom? Did Leonard say?"

"No, not yet," she said, reaching for her coffee cup.

The boy poured a tumbler full of milk, then downed half of it before he decided to put the container back in the refrigerator. "I sure hope it isn't Dan. Last year was the pits, with him yelling and giving orders all the time. Some of the guys didn't want to play this year because of him."

Natalie eyed her son thoughtfully. Bryon had always been a quiet boy who respected his elders. She couldn't remember him speaking out against Dan Jenkins at all during last year's season, although she knew he'd wanted to. Apparently, Dan Jenkins had made a bad impression with more people than just herself. She smiled reassuringly. "Don't worry, honey. Dan won't be on our team."

"How'd ya know that?"

She lifted one shoulder, hesitating to admit that she'd gone so far as to speak to Leonard about the problem. "He was on our team last year. We'll have someone different this time," she said.

"Can I have a bite?" he asked as he watched his mother slice into the piece of cake.

"May I?" she gently corrected.

"May I?" he repeated obediently.

She passed the forkful of cake to him and smiled as it disappeared in one bite. "Your grandmother said you've already eaten three pieces," she reminded him.

"Yeah, but it's good."

He gulped down the rest of the milk. "Jimmy's dad was gonna offer to coach this year. He'd be real good. But they changed him to the late shift on his job."

"Oh, that's too bad," Natalie said, "and you're right, he would have been good." Jimmy was one of Bryon's best friends. He lived only two blocks from Natalie and Bryon. His father worked for the Grand River Dam Authority, a generating plant just a few miles from town.

Natalie drained the rest of her coffee, then rose and placed her cup and plate in the sink. "You'd better go and take your bath. It's almost bedtime."

"Two more minutes," he pleaded.

Smiling to herself, she shook her head. "What good are two more minutes?"

He shrugged and brushed back the dark hair falling across his forehead. "It's just two more minutes."

"Until surrender, you mean?" she joked.

"Aw, Mom," he groaned and slowly rose from the chair.

He was growing up in a hurry. She supposed she was like most parents. They loved seeing their children grow, but they hated losing the child in them, too. Many times Natalie had doubted her ability to be both mother and father to Bryon, but since James died, she had devoted all the time she wasn't working to her son. He was a good boy, one to be proud of.

"Bryon," she said, just as he started to disappear through the door.

"Yes?"

She wiped her hands on a dish towel and looked at him. "Does it embarrass you to have your mother coaching?"

His young face wrinkled with confusion. "No. Why are you asking such a dumb question? All the other guys think it's neat that I have a mom who knows all about baseball."

Natalie smiled faintly. "And what about you? Do you think it's neat?"

"No, I think it's great!" he exclaimed. Before she could say anything else, he'd trotted out the door. "Good night, Mom," he called back down the hallway.

"Good night."

With a contented smile, Natalie locked the door and switched off the lights. Poor Louise, she thought. The woman was so set in her ideas. Natalie didn't intentionally do things to irritate her. It was just that there weren't many things that didn't irritate her mother-in-law.

Now Harvey, her father-in-law, was a different matter altogether. He rarely had anything to say one way or the other. Natalie believed that was because Louise's forceful personality canceled his out.

Well, she thought, feeling tired, a few more years and Bryon would be grown. Things would be different then.

Things would be different—the words rolled over in her mind as she walked into her bedroom. How different? she wondered.

Stepping into the bathroom, after Bryon had finished his bath, she began to undress. She'd had a hard day today. The dull ache between her shoulders reminded her how tired she really was.

That was it, she decided. That was why these restless, depressing moods seemed to sweep over her lately. There was nothing wrong with her life the way it was. She had a wonderful son, a nice, comfortable house, a good job in a department store in Muskogee, good health, and although her finances weren't formidable, they weren't shaky, either.

So why are you suddenly looking at yourself in the mirror and wondering where the years have gone, wondering where you're headed? she asked herself. Was it because she'd looked at that cowboy tonight and was uncharacteristically stirred by his appeal?

Telling herself the question didn't warrant an answer, she tossed the pile of clothes at her feet into the wicker hamper and stepped into the shower.

A few minutes later, she entered the bedroom feeling refreshed. Securing the towel that was knotted just above her breasts, she sat on the stool in front of her dressing table.

Her wet, auburn hair was tangled. She picked up a wide-toothed comb and slowly slicked the long, wavy strands away from her face.

A beautiful woman stared back at her, but Natalie did not recognize the full power of her appearance. She saw only the fine lines fanning out from the corners of her green eyes, the subtle hints of aging in her porcelain complexion and the full, mature look of her body.

Is that it, Natalie? Are you depressed because you're thirty-three, not twenty-five? Angry at the little voice inside her head, she snatched a jar of moisturizer from the dressing table.

Of course she wasn't depressed because of her age, she told herself as she patted the cream around her eyes. She wasn't one of those women who wanted to stay young forever, one of those women who lived only to attract men.

Men. The word had become almost foreign to her. She shuddered as it entered her thoughts. She didn't allow herself to think about men—not because she didn't like them, far from it, actually. She got along with men quite well in the workplace, but that was as far as it went. Men had no place in her private life.

Not too long after James died, several men had tried to date Natalie, but James's memory got in the way. Later, she just didn't know. She'd found a couple of men attractive, yet as soon as she realized she was attracted to them, she'd been so overwhelmed with guilt that she'd cut them out of her life. She had married James at an early age and he'd been the only man in her life. She'd felt it would have been disrespectful to his memory to put it all behind her and build a new life with another man.

As time fell away behind her, though, Natalie began to realize that way of thinking had been a bit extreme. Yet even knowing this, she had been reluctant to have another man in her life. James had been steady and predictable. There was so much involved, so much at stake when two people shared a relationship—especially when a child was involved. Would she be able to deal with someone different? Did she really want to? Eventually, Natalie spent so much time weighing and asking herself these questions that the answers no longer mattered. She had been alone for so long now that she'd come to accept sharing herself only with her son. Bryon was her life and right now she wasn't going to think about him growing up and moving away from her.

She rose from the dressing table, walked over and turned down the bed covers, then switched off the lamp on the bedside table. With the room thrust into sudden darkness, she loosened the knot between her breast and let the damp towel fall to the floor.

The glow of the street lamp filtering through the curtains barely lit the soft curves of her body as she climbed between the bed covers and closed her eyes.

The image of a man quickly invaded the black haven behind her lids. She felt something like fear, and her eyes flew open in an effort to shake the mental picture. This had never happened to her before, she thought with a little panic. Why should it happen now?

You know why it's happening, she told herself. *That handsome cowboy you met this evening has reminded you that you still have a woman's needs.*

No, she thought fiercely. He was just some young guy who enjoyed a little flirtation. She groaned at the word. Flirtation, is that what it had been? She didn't really know any more. It had been so long since she'd even thought about such things. Besides, what in the world made her think he would actually give her a second look? The man was gorgeous. All he probably had to do was crook a finger and women would come running.

You're losing it, Natalie, she told herself, *letting your imagination be dominated by a stranger.* It was a good thing baseball season was starting. She needed a diversion. That was all, she assured herself. Just a diversion. In a few days she would probably find this whole episode amusing.

Determinedly, she pulled the sheets up under her chin and settled her head more comfortably against the pillows. She was afraid to close her eyes. She was afraid his image would reappear. The man with blue eyes, tanned skin and a cowboy hat. A man she didn't even know.

Chapter Two

I'd rather just have my money back. If I can't have that color, I don't want it!"

Natalie looked at the woman standing in front of the checkout counter and tried to hide her impatience. "And what did you say was wrong with the blouse?"

The older woman drew in a breath as if she considered Natalie's question an insult. "It's too small."

Discreetly, Natalie glanced at the tag in the back of the collar. No wonder, she thought. The woman should be in the queen-size shop instead of trying to squeeze into junior clothing. "Did you look on the rack to make sure there wasn't a larger one in this color?"

The woman gave her a curt nod. "I certainly did! I also asked the clerk if there were any in stock."

Natalie forced herself to smile even though her legs were hurting and it was past time for her to go home. "Of course, we'll be glad to give you a refund. But I'll have to fill out a form for you to sign."

Why did things have to go wrong today, when she needed to get home early? She groaned silently. Rummaging through files beneath the counter, Natalie found the refund slips. As she filled in the spaces, she glanced around for her co-worker. Of all the times—Dana was going to be late because of a dental appointment. And on top of everything else, a blasted refund.

The disgruntled customer was counting her money and walking away when Dana finally appeared behind the work counter. "You're still here!" she exclaimed, glancing at her wristwatch.

Natalie grimaced at the young blonde. "Where else would I be?"

"I thought Jerry could watch this part until I returned."

Jerry was a young man who worked the men's department. "Jerry's been swamped. I couldn't leave."

"Gosh, I'm sorry, Nattie. Baseball starts today, doesn't it?"

Natalie nodded as she quickly gathered up her purse and a few other odds and ends she'd brought to work. "Right. And if I don't get home there's going to be fifteen or twenty boys wondering what's happened to their coach."

"One is going to be wondering what's happened to his mother."

"Oh, gosh," Natalie moaned. "Dana, would you be a dear and give Bryon a call? Tell him I'm on my way."

"Sure thing. Now get out of here, but drive safely. It won't help matters if you're caught speeding."

Natalie waved goodbye to Dana and started in a run toward the big double doors of the department store. "I will. See you tomorrow."

Traffic was terrible. But then it always was at five-thirty in the evening. The highway between Muskogee and Fort Gibson was filled with workers going home for the day.

Natalie impatiently weaved in and out of traffic, picking up speed when an opening allowed it. Spring was in full force. If she hadn't been in such a hurry she would have enjoyed the four-mile drive. Forsythia and jonquils added bright yellow to the landscape, along with red fire bushes and Persian lilacs. Most of the terrain around Muskogee was flat farmland, but farther north, past Fort Gibson and on toward Talequah, lay rolling, wooded hills.

Fort Gibson was an old town, in fact the oldest in the state. When Oklahoma was still Indian territory, the Fort Gibson stockade had housed army troops, then later, during the Civil War, was the headquarters of the Union Army. The stockade was still standing, having been reconstructed during the 1930s. Thousands of tourists visited the military park each year to learn about the history of the area and how the Cherokees, Seminoles and Cree had found Fort Gibson, the last leg on their Trail of Tears.

But the historical flavor of the town was not the only reason Natalie liked it. She liked the small, friendly size of it, the old buildings that seemed to assure a person that many things did and could endure. She enjoyed the slow, laid-back life-style, the shaded streets, the front porches where rockers or lawn chairs were rarely vacant.

It was ironic that after years of being dragged from one army base to another, she had wound up living only three blocks from an old fort. Her father, Douglas Winfield, still served as a major in the army. At the moment, he and her mother, Phyllis, were stationed in Hawaii, just one of a long list of places they'd lived over the years.

Natalie didn't miss army life. Quite the contrary. It was wonderful not to have her roots constantly pulled up and be moved to a strange place, even if Louise did grate on her nerves at times.

"Mom, hurry! We're going to be late!" Bryon exclaimed as he met his mother out on the small front porch.

"Yes, I know, darling. Just let me go change. Will you get some cans of soda out of the pantry and throw them with some ice into the cooler?"

"Sure, just hurry."

Natalie trotted down the hall to her bedroom and quickly stripped off her yellow print skirt. She was wearing a yellow cotton shirt, so she left it on and added a pair of navy blue shorts. By the time she'd tied the shoelaces of a pair of tennis shoes and had entered the living room, Bryon was lugging the ice chest out the front door.

After loading it into the back of Natalie's Nissan, they were headed toward the ballpark.

"Did Dana call and tell you I'd be late?" Natalie asked after she'd taken a deep, relaxing breath.

"Yes. Leonard called, too."

Natalie's dark brows rose. "What did he want?"

"Just to see if you would be able to make it this evening and that a Mr. Tanner, or something like that, would be the other coach."

Natalie's face wrinkled in confusion. "Mr. Tanner? Are you sure? I don't know anyone by that name."

Bryon shrugged as he slammed his fist into his glove with eager anticipation. "All I know is what he told me. As long as it's not Dan Jenkins, I don't care."

"I'm inclined to agree with you," she said. "But honey, don't say anything like that to the other boys, okay? We wouldn't want Mr. Jenkins's feelings hurt by any kind of talk."

"Don't worry, Mom. I won't say anything," he promised.

Natalie smiled and reached across the seat to ruffle his hair affectionately. "You ready to play?"

"I'm ready!" he yelped with excitement.

There were several cars and pickups parked outside the wire fence surrounding the baseball diamond. Boys in everything from tank tops and shorts to sweatshirts and jeans were milling around on the field.

Natalie drove her little white car next to the vehicle on the end and braked it to a sudden halt.

"Oh, my gosh, Bryon. We've forgotten the equipment!" she groaned as she switched off the motor.

"No, we didn't," Bryon assured her, already climbing out of the car. "Leonard said that Mr. Tanner would have it."

For the second time Natalie's brows arched over her almond-shaped eyes. It sounded like Mr. Tanner was already into the swing of things. "Oh, he did? You didn't tell me."

"I forgot. We were in a hurry, remember?" he said, defending himself.

"It's just as well." Natalie groaned. "This hasn't exactly been my day." Usually she was very organized and punctual. Rushing to practice and already late—it wasn't like her at all.

Bryon took off in a run toward the group of boys gathered behind home plate. Suddenly he pulled up short and glanced back at his mother, who was following at a more sedate pace. "Mom, what about the ice chest? Did you want to unload it now?"

Natalie shook her head. "Go on. It's for after practice."

"Hey, Natalie, you gonna win the championship this year?"

Natalie turned her head at the sound of a male voice. Glancing up in the bleachers she saw Ray Whitefield and his wife, Gena. They were friends of Louise and Harvey's and had a grandson who was Bryon's age. Obviously Randy was going to be on her team this year.

"I'm going to try," she assured the couple with a cheery smile.

"I don't envy you," Gena spoke up. "Looks like you have a big group of boys this year."

Natalie glanced toward the crowd on the field. There were a lot of youngsters, but that wasn't what she first noticed. Standing in the midst of the boys was a young man who looked vaguely familiar. His hair was dark blond and stuck out in unruly curls beneath a navy blue baseball cap. The shoulders under the white T-shirt were broad and thick despite the overall leanness of his body. She didn't know him, but still... Glancing back at Ray and Gena, she said, "Looks like I better get to work. See you later."

They waved as Natalie hurried around the heavy wire backstop.

"Hi, Natalie. How ya doin'?"

Natalie turned again at the sound of the greeting. A young woman relaxing in a lawn chair next to the fence was waving at her.

"Hi, Linda. Is Jeremy playing this year?"

The young woman pointed toward the group of boys. "He's in there somewhere. I can assure you he's excited about being on your team. You have a reputation among the boys.''

Natalie laughed, a rich warm sound. "I always did want a reputation," she joked.

By then most of the boys had spotted her. A chorus of voices split the air. "Hi, Mrs. Fuller."

Natalie walked slowly toward the group of boys and the man who was to be her assistant. She knew nearly every boy present and she greeted each of them by name until she came to the man. When her eyes met his, she realized where she'd seen him before. Oh, no! she thought. She'd been teamed with the stranger from the meeting!

He gave her a wide, friendly smile and extended his hand toward her. "Hello, I guess you're Natalie Fuller," he said.

She nodded and found herself smiling at him even though she felt frozen in surprise. Lifting her hand, she allowed his strong, callused fingers to close around it. "You guessed right. And you must be Mr. Tanner?''

He nodded. "Just Matt or Matthew to you, ma'am."

Natalie wondered how long he was going to keep holding her hand. Why did looking into his blue, blue eyes make her stomach feel as though it hadn't seen food in two days? "Please call me Natalie," she said. "After all, we'll be working together for a while."

He loosened his grip on her hand. She let out a pent-up breath just as he said, "I've got to admit I thought Leonard Tully was playing a trick on me when he said my partner would be a lady. But the boys here assure me you're a great coach."

"Thanks to three brothers and no sisters, I grew up playing baseball instead of having tea parties. At least all that time is paying off now, in spite of my mother's disapproval back then.''

He chuckled at her admission, then looked down as a young boy of about ten tugged on his elbow. "Hey, Mr. Tanner, can I try out for catcher?''

"Have you ever played catcher?'' he asked.

The boy, whose name was Casey, nodded his head. "At home. With my friends.''

Natalie was impressed to see Matt Tanner giving his full attention to the child. With fifteen or twenty youngsters, it was difficult to work one on one. Natalie always tried to keep in mind that each boy was an individual, and that in their young hearts playing on this baseball team was to them like playing in the Major Leagues.

"Catching is a hard job," Matt stated. "It takes a lot of work and practice. Think you can handle it?''

The boy nodded his fiery red head emphatically. "I'll practice real hard!''

"Okay, we'll see what you can do later on.''

Casey grinned broadly and let out a loud yelp as he trotted back to the group of milling boys.

"I think you just made his day." Natalie smiled as she watched Casey do the high five with some of his friends.

"It's been a long time, but I can still remember how it was," he replied, tossing her a reflective smile.

Natalie looked at his darkly tanned face. He was good-looking—she'd seen it in just those few moments the other night at the meeting. In the light of day it was even more evident to her. But she had to admit that his attractiveness was not only due to the well-arranged features of his face. It was a combination of many things—his dark, smooth skin, sky-blue eyes and the crooked grin that revealed teeth so perfect and white they flashed against his skin. There was a healthy sheen to his thick blond hair and she knew the tousled curls tickling the back of his neck were natural. All in all, he exuded a sexy virility that Natalie had never noticed in another man.

The whole idea embarrassed her. She hadn't been attracted to a man in years, and here she was looking at this one, her heart thumping with unusual vigor. *For God's sake, Natalie,* she scolded herself. *We're in front of a bunch of boys and several parents. Act your age,* her mind chided.

"I don't think it's been all that long since you've played baseball," she said, almost in an effort to make her remember she was looking at a man who was younger than herself—by several years, she'd guess.

He chuckled. The sound was low and warm. "Don't you believe it. I've been on the rodeo circuit for the past eight years. That doesn't leave time for baseball, or anything else."

Natalie continued to look at him and found herself wanting to ask him all sorts of questions about his life— where was he going, where had he been and where was he headed? But now was not the time, she reminded herself, nor would any time be. They were here to practice baseball and nothing else. It made her angry to realize that for the first time in a long time, she was curious about a man.

"I'm sure you'll get right back in the swing of things," she said, glancing away from him and to the boys, who were looking bored and impatient. "I think we'd better get started before we have a riot on our hands."

"I think you're right. And since you've done this before, why don't we go along with your regular routine," he suggested.

One thing about it, she thought. Matt Tanner was definitely not going to be another Dan Jenkins. She was thankful for that much, at least.

She looked up at him, hoping her expression was purely businesslike. "Well, I usually divide them into pairs and let them limber up by playing catch first. I don't know too much about pitching, so if you do, you might want to select two or three boys you think would be good at it."

Matt Tanner nodded as he looked at Natalie. His surprise at having being paired with a woman coach had worn off—until he'd seen her walk out onto the field. He'd known immediately that she was the woman he'd sat behind on the night of the meeting. For more than an hour, he'd gazed at her back, wondering what kind of face could be attached to such a beautiful, full head of auburn hair. It was thick and curly and fell against the regal set of her small shoulders. The silken mass had reminded Matt of the glow of a dark flame. Bored with the meeting, he'd sat there drawing imaginary features to go with the hair. His imaginings hadn't even come close to the beauty he'd discovered when she turned and looked at him. Ivory skin, pale green eyes, soft generous lips and dimpled chin. The combination had bowled him over completely.

Now she was here in front of him again. In spite of himself, he was wondering about her. She had a son, but there was no wedding ring on her left hand. *So Matt Tanner, what are you going to do about it?* he thought to himself wryly. *Ask her outright if she's married? Don't be a damned idiot! You're in front of a crowd. This isn't the time or place. Besides,* he argued with the voice in his head, *she's not your type at all. Liar,* the voice taunted.

"Fine," he said with a smile. "Let's get the equipment out and see if we can get these boys started."

Natalie took a deep breath to steady herself, and followed him to the pitcher's mound and the crowd of rowdy boys.

For the next half hour, Matt learned the boys' names and gave them tips on throwing and catching the baseball properly. Matt chose three older boys he thought would be suitable for pitching and took them aside to work with them separately. Natalie took the other fifteen and had them practice their fielding skills.

It was growing dark and the air had begun to cool by the time they brought the practice to an end.

When Bryon reminded his mother of the soda in the trunk of the car, Matt offered to carry it to the bleachers for her. He even helped her fill the paper cups with ice and distribute the drinks among the boys.

Most of the parents who had stayed to watch the practice were in a rush to get home, so the greater part of the team was gone by the time Natalie sat down on one of the wooden bleachers to enjoy her drink. Bryon and a few boys who had come to practice on bicycles were sitting on the grass behind the backstop.

Matt was speaking to one of the fathers. Natalie studied him furtively beneath her thick lashes. All during practice she'd been aware of him, even when he was far across the field. She kept asking herself the same questions over and over: Why was he offering to coach a bunch of young boys? Where did he live? What did he do?

He'd mentioned being in the rodeo, but only in the past tense, as though he didn't do it anymore. Her eyes left his face and followed the lines of his long, lean legs in the faded jeans. The corners of her mouth lifted slightly as

she noticed the brown cowboy boots on his feet. He
hadn't deserted the rodeo image, she thought.

There were lots of cowboys around Fort Gibson, since
farming and ranching were widespread in the area. Natalie had never known a cowboy personally, however.
They were a very different breed from the people she associated with. She'd always been a city or town girl, and
so had her friends and family. Now, as she studied Matt's
hard-muscled frame, she wondered about his life-style.
Any sport in rodeo would take a lot of skill and
strength—she did know that much. Judging by the look
of his body, Matt Tanner had plenty of both. He had that
weathered look about him—a look that told her he'd
been taking care of himself for a long time and the road
he'd been down hadn't always been easy. But something
else told her that along the way he'd known a few women.
Normally, she despised that air of experience in a man.
But on Matt Tanner, it only seemed to heighten his appeal. He was like forbidden fruit.

Her thoughts about the man came to an abrupt halt as
she watched him bid farewell to the other man. He
walked toward the bleachers and her.

"Well, how do you think it went?" he asked.

Natalie took a sip of her drink and tried to appear calm
and casual—something that was usually very easy for her.
But not now. Not with this man standing in front of her,
exuding sensuality.

"I think it went fine, don't you? I believe we've got a
great bunch of kids. Most of them handle the ball very
well."

He lifted his right boot and planted it smoothly on the
bottom bleacher. "You're right. I'm looking forward to
the season."

His blue gaze settled on her face and she felt her blood warm and spread its heat throughout her body. Lord, why couldn't she react normally to this man? She wasn't some kind of frustrated widow or divorcée. Why was she suddenly bombarded with all kinds of ridiculous feelings? If Matt Tanner knew what was running through her mind, he'd probably laugh. She was years older than he was; he'd never be attracted to her. She was the mother of an eleven-year-old son, for Pete's sake. Matt could have any young woman he wanted. He certainly wouldn't look at someone like her . . . but he *was* looking, and she was looking back.

"You'll probably change your mind when the temperature gets around a hundred, the boys are fussing and we haven't won any games."

He chuckled softly. "It can't be all that bad. If I thought it would be, I wouldn't have let Leonard talk me into it."

She couldn't hide her curiosity. "You know Leonard?"

He nodded, lifting the ball cap from his head and thrusting his fingers through his hair. "From way back. He lives out by my grandparents."

"Oh. So you have folks that live in the area?"

He nodded. "About three miles north of town. My grandfather owns a fairly large farm, and since he's grown too old to manage it on his own, I've come back home to help him."

Back home, she thought. This had once been his home. "So you're farming now?"

"Yes. Corn, soybeans, a little alfalfa."

His eyes were focused on her lips. Self-consciously, she licked them, knowing that the pale peach color she'd applied this afternoon was long gone by now. In an effort to keep her thoughts on more sensible things, she asked, "Do you like it?"

"Like what?" he asked lazily. "Living here or farming?"

"Farming." She wondered how on earth he could make a plain white T-shirt look so good. Natalie had always liked a man to be well-dressed. Slacks, dress shirts, nice conservative ties. As she looked at this man, she realized that James had never affected her like Matt did, but on the other hand, James hadn't been like Matt at all. He'd never worn jeans or boots or anything as casual as a T-shirt. His skin had never been baked by the sun and wind; his hands had never been rough and callused as Matt's were. James had devoted his life to the indoor world of helping people survive illnesses and accidents. He had spent time almost exclusively in the rooms and corridors of a hospital. But Matt Tanner was earthy—a man's man. His roof was the sky, the soil his livelihood. He worked with and against the weather, always battling things he couldn't control, and when he was lucky, he won. She knew he was the type of man who enjoyed the risk and adventure of it all.

"I love farming," he said. "It's hard work, but it's a challenge."

"And you like being challenged?"

One corner of his mouth lifted and he rested his forearm across his raised knee. "I'd be bored to death without it."

She took a deep breath and released it haltingly. "Yes, I believe you would be."

Matt watched her fingers lift and toy nervously with a curl near her temple. "What about you, Natalie? Do you live a challenging life?"

Her head shook briefly. "I live a very safe and boring life. Six in the morning to ten in the evening—that's the extent of it."

His smile was a bit twisted, as if he didn't quite believe her. "A lot can happen between six and ten."

Natalie had flirted with men before. She knew all the signs and they were not written on Matt Tanner's face, in spite of the twinkle in his eye. He was merely making a statement, and his expression showed that he found life so enjoyable that he thought everyone else did, too.

She laughed softly and sipped her drink. "Well, being a mother is exciting at times. Bryon has had all kinds of cuts and bruises. And he's brought home all sorts of strange animals. Things can get crazy at times."

In the distance she saw the boys slowly getting to their feet and ambling off toward their bicycles. Bryon tossed his paper cup into a trash barrel at the end of the bleachers, then headed toward her and Matt.

"Hey, Mr. Tanner, you sure can throw a baseball. Did you play in high school?" Bryon asked. He scrambled up beside his mother.

Matt grinned at the boy. "Sure did. Played in college, too."

Natalie glanced at Matt in surprise. She hadn't expected him to be a college graduate. But then, there were probably a lot of surprising things about him.

"Really," Bryon exclaimed. "Where'd you go to college?"

"Bryon, you're being nosy," Natalie admonished her son. He was always friendly with people, but not to this extent. It was obvious he liked Matthew Tanner.

Matt ignored Natalie. "I went to OSU so I could study agriculture and play baseball."

"You played ball there! Boy, you must have been good. OSU is nearly always in the College World Series," Bryon said, his brown eyes wide.

Matt shook his head with a laugh. "No, I wasn't that good. But I tried hard, so I got to travel with the team."

"Wow! That must have been great!"

"Well, maybe you can do it, too, someday," Matt told him. "You've just gotta stay with it and keep practicing. Does your dad know as much about baseball as your mother? If he does, you're bound to be a winner."

Suddenly, Bryon was at a loss for words and Natalie hurried to his rescue. "Bryon's father died several years ago."

Matt looked from Natalie back to Bryon. The expression on his features showed them that he was very sorry. "That's too bad, son," he said. He reached over and scuffed the top of Bryon's head. "But you still have an edge on the other guys. Your mom's the coach. So make her practice with you all the time."

Bryon laughed, his usual good spirits returning. "I will."

Trying to seem purposeful, Natalie rose to her feet. The three were the only ones left at the ballpark. She and Bryon needed to get home. "It's getting late. We'd better be going, Bryon."

Matt glanced at his wristwatch. "You're right. It's after eight. I sure hope Granny took pity on me and fed the chickens."

"Chickens!" Bryon echoed as he jumped down from the bleachers. "You raise chickens?"

Matt laughed. He strode easily beside Natalie and Bryon. "No, I raise the crops. My grandmother raises the chickens. Says it makes her feel good to be awakened every morning by a rooster."

"I've got a radio that wakes me up," Bryon told him. "But it doesn't feel good to be woken up by it."

Matt looked over at Natalie and winked. "Maybe your mother should get you a rooster."

Natalie smiled dryly. "I don't think the neighbors would agree."

They had reached Natalie's car. Matt's black truck was parked on the other side of the field. He'd obviously escorted them to the car out of politeness.

"Well, good night," he told them after Natalie had climbed behind the wheel and Bryon had joined her on the passenger side of the car. "See you Tuesday. I'll bring the drinks."

He was leaning down near the window. Natalie looked up at him in surprise. "It's kind of you to offer, but I don't mind."

"Nonsense," he insisted. "We'll take turns. That's only fair. And Bryon," he added, glancing across at the boy, "see if you can talk your mother into letting you come out to the farm sometime. There's a pond you can fish in, big tractors and horses to ride, dogs, cats and a lot more fun stuff."

"Gee, can I, Mom?" Bryon asked eagerly.

Natalie couldn't believe her ears. Bryon had never responded so warmly to anyone as quickly as this. Wariness coursed through her. Bryon was a sensitive boy. She hoped Matt wasn't leading him on for her benefit.

Don't be ridiculous, Natalie, she furiously chided herself. Matt Tanner wasn't a sneaky womanizer. He was merely a nice man offering a boy without a father the chance to visit a farm.

"We'll see," she told her son. "Now tell Mr. Tanner good-night."

"Good night, Mr. Tanner," Bryon echoed happily.

As Natalie started the engine of her little sports car, Matt stepped away from the window and waved a casual farewell.

Bryon talked about him all the way home, but thoughts of Matt Tanner didn't end there for Natalie. They stayed with her all through the night.

Chapter Three

Granny, she's the prettiest thing I've ever seen."

Claudie Tanner turned from the kitchen sink to cast an eye at her grandson. "That's quite a statement, coming from you, Matt. You've known a bunch of pretty girls down through the years."

Matt raised his glass of iced tea to his lips. He took a long drink before looking at his grandmother. She was a short woman, barely five feet tall, with thick white hair and a figure made plump by a steady diet of home cooking. At seventy, she could still keep up with the best of them. She kept her own vegetable garden, did all the housecleaning and cooking. She had been more of a mother to him than her daughter-in-law had ever been. Claudie and Amos Tanner had been the foundation of his life—especially when his parents got divorced. He'd been ten at the time, but even at that tender age the divorce hadn't come as a surprise.

His father, Jared, was a gambler and an adventurer. Sandy, his mother, was one of those women who loved excitement and fast times. Together, they'd lived a life with more ups and downs than a roller-coaster ride, For the first nine years of Matt's life, he'd been dragged from racetrack to racetrack, from casino to casino, living out of cheap motels or, at best, spending two or three months in a rented house. That is, until Claudie and Amos had demanded their grandson have a permanent home where he could attend a proper school.

Looking at his grandmother now, he realized everything good and decent in him was because of his grandparents. He loved them as much as life itself.

Placing the iced tea on the kitchen table, he bent to kiss her freckled cheek. "Yeah, but none of those women were as pretty as you, Granny."

She clucked her tongue and lovingly pushed him away. "Hush your nonsense and tell me more about the one that's caught your fancy."

He leaned his tall, wiry frame against the cabinets and watched Claudie peel the turnips. "Well, like I said, she's the prettiest thing I've ever seen. She has soft ivory skin, pale green eyes and dark red hair. And one of those sweet little dimpled chins."

Claudie arched an eyebrow at him. "That just tells me about the outside. What about the inside?"

Matt shrugged and slipped a slice of turnip from the pan before his grandmother could rap him on the wrist. "I don't know," he admitted, crunching into the raw turnip. "I just met her on Friday. She has a son. He's eleven. Her husband has been dead for several years."

"She's a widow, then," Claudie commented.

Matt nodded. "Yeah, and that isn't like me, is it?"

Claudie shook her head, but there was a wry little smile on her face. "No," she agreed. "But stranger things have happened."

"Well, there's nothing wrong with being a widow, is there?"

"No. Couldn't have been of her choosin'."

Matt swallowed the rest of his turnip. "She's kind of reserved, Granny. I don't know if that's her personality or if that's just the way she is around strangers. Anyway, she's real good with the boys. They seem to love her."

"How is she as a coach?"

"She knows what she's doing."

"Fuller," Claudie repeated aloud. I don't believe I know any Fullers."

Matt pushed himself away from the cabinets. "I don't believe they move in our circles, Granny. The kind of clothes she wears don't speak of farming or hard labor."

Claudie cast a doubtful glance at him. "Are you sure this woman would suit you?"

Matt grinned at his grandmother. "No. But I'm sure as heck going to find out."

The sun was still strong and hot when Matt carried a cooler filled with colas, ice and a bag of homemade cookies out to his pickup.

About a hundred yards away, down in the pasture, Amos, his grandfather, cast his fishing line into a pond filled with lily pads. Matt waved at him as he backed out of the drive.

In his early seventies, Amos was still a strong, healthy man. But the last couple of years he had decided it was about time he stopped working eight to ten hours a day. Matthew supposed his grandfather had put off retiring until he was sure his grandson was ready to settle down to farming.

One corner of Matt's mouth lifted as he thought about the past five or six months of his life. Farming was a slow, predictable life compared to traveling across the country to several rodeos a week. A person ran into all kinds of adventures along the way. Especially when he traveled with a partner.

Matthew had worked the team roping event—one man would rope a steer around the horns and the other would rope the two hind legs. Success depended on both partners and their mounts. It was a precision sport, requiring skill and perfect timing. Coordinating two ropers, two horses and a steer that was trying his best to get away wasn't an easy feat. Matt had lost his share of money over the years, but he'd also won his share, too. It had been a good life for him, one that he learned from and enjoyed.

His partner, Lyle, was still trying to get him back on the circuit, but Matt's mind was made up. Although the rodeo life had been exciting and enjoyable, he was ready to give it up and settle down. In a strange sort of way, Lyle had been a contributing factor to Matt's decision. He was a married man with two daughters. But since he was away so much of the time, Lyle's daughters were growing up without him, and his wife was growing away from him. Matt didn't want that type of life. If he was ever lucky enough to have a wife and children, he wanted them to know they were the most important thing in his life. And he knew they would be.

But Matt had never been able to get that kind of reasoning through to his partner. It both saddened and frustrated him, because Lyle had been a good friend for many years. Matt wanted him to be happy. But they were different men with different goals in life. Matt had already attained the one that Lyle kept wanting. Now Matt wanted more—a home, a family of his own, time to spend with his grandparents while they were still alive and well.

As the farmland flew by him and the outskirts of Fort Gibson appeared, Matt's thoughts turned to Natalie Fuller. The attraction he felt for her still came as a surprise. As Claudie had said, Natalie wasn't at all like any of the women he'd dated in the past. That wasn't only because she was a widow with a child. All the women he'd ever been involved with were much younger than he was—usually several years younger. Not that age had had anything to do with it, he told himself. He just hadn't been looking for anything permanent. He had purposely dated women who didn't want to be tied down. But now... *Well, hell, Matt,* he silently cursed. *What makes you think Natalie Fuller would want anything permanent, either? Especially with someone like you?*

The question still rankled him as he pulled up at the ball field. But the niggling doubts suddenly vanished as he spotted Natalie in a pair of white shorts and a vivid turquoise blouse. She was weaving in and out of the group of boys. Yes, she was right for him, he thought, watching her. From the moment he'd looked at her face, he'd known she was the woman for him. Sooner or later, he was going to let her know it, too.

"Are you guys early or am I late?" he asked the boys as they crowded around him and the two duffel bags of equipment he carried.

Natalie stopped. She found herself staring at Matt. She'd remembered how good-looking he was, but she had forgotten just how vibrant and distracting his presence was to her.

Even now, in a crowd, she couldn't force her eyes away from him. It was as if she hadn't seen him in weeks, instead of days.

The boys began to dig into the bags and pulled out baseballs, bats and other gear. Matt glanced at Natalie and smiled.

"How are you today, Natalie?"

She felt herself smiling warmly back at him, in spite of many inner warnings. "I'm fine. Bryon and I managed to make it on time today, thankfully."

"That's good. How was your weekend?"

Natalie didn't see what that had to do with baseball, but she didn't care. She'd thought about him all weekend and now it was so good to see him again, she didn't mind him getting a little personal. "It was very nice. The weather has been beautiful, don't you think?"

"Very beautiful. I've already managed to get most of my corn planted. So I'm ready for a little rain."

Natalie looked up at the sky, grateful to see the sun was going to set in a clear sky. "Baseball and rain don't mix too well," she said.

Laughingly, he agreed. "I'll only wish for a little. Just enough to get the corn growing."

She smiled at his teasing manner. "And what about baseball?"

By now he had maneuvered himself through the boys and was standing beside her. Natalie caught the earthy scent clinging to his skin and clothes. It brought erotic thoughts to her mind; thoughts she had been sure had died long ago.

"I'll ask the big man to hold off on game days," he said, motioning toward the heavens.

Natalie gave him a sidelong glance. "Are your prayers always answered?"

She expected a teasing grin to cross his face. Natalie was surprised to see a serious expression on his face as he looked at her. "So far."

She took a deep breath and felt his eyes drawn to the thrust of her breasts as they rose and fell beneath her cotton blouse.

Had other men looked at her like this man did? she wondered, or was she only noticing it now? Whatever the answer, she hoped God would hear her prayer. She had to get through this time with Matt without making a fool of herself. She already felt like a fool. She was reacting to him like a love-starved widow who hadn't encountered a man for years, she thought angrily. If her friends or family knew what she was thinking, they'd laugh themselves silly. Natalie probably would have, too, if it didn't all feel quite so serious.

"Well," she said in an effort to bring her thoughts back to business, "should we pair the boys off and let them warm up?"

"I'm ready. Are you boys ready?" He directed his question to the group.

A chorus of rowdy approval was the response. Leather mitts and a few stray baseballs were tossed into the air. There was much shouting and jumping up and down before the boys paired themselves off and got busy tossing the balls back and forth.

Natalie stood to one side, studying each boy's abilities, while Matt carried the equipment that had been left out on the field and piled it next to the backstop.

When he was finished, he joined Natalie. For a moment he didn't say anything and Natalie wondered if she should suggest what to do with the rest of the practice period. But she hesitated, not wanting him to think she was trying to play the big shot.

He took the problem out of her hands by saying, "I think I'll take Ron, Steve and Billy over to one side and work on their pitching. What do you think we should do with the rest of the group?"

In the past, Natalie had never felt at a loss on the baseball field. She'd always known what she wanted the boys to do and learn—and how and when she wanted them to learn it. Now her mind seemed to be a blank. Too busy thinking about seeing Matt again, she hadn't even made any plans for the practice.

"I think I'll knock them a few grounders and see how their fielding is. I know they're all anxious to bat, so let's leave that for the last. What do you think?"

"Hey, you're the boss." He grinned. "I'm just the assistant."

Her brows arched. "Don't say that. I need a partner."

He grinned lopsidedly and she felt the crazy thump of her heart start up all over again. "Is it as bad as that?" he asked.

She nodded. "Especially when you have eighteen eager little faces and only nine starting positions."

To her utter surprise he reached over and gave her shoulder an encouraging squeeze. "Don't worry. If you want, I'll name the starters. That way, if anyone gets angry or hurt, they can take it out on me."

Natalie blushed. She shook back her red curls and looked at him through lowered lashes. "I guess you think I don't like to stick my neck out?"

He shook his head and his hand fell from her slender shoulder. "No, I just think you've got a soft heart."

"And you don't?"

The grin left his face. Only the corners of his mouth remained faintly tilted. "Let's just say my exterior is a bit tougher than yours."

That was quite an understatement, he thought, eyeing her womanly curves. She had the kind of body that constantly reminded a man he was a man.

As he looked at her rosy cheeks, he wondered what kind of life she led. Did she date often? Or was she more interested in a career? He didn't even know if she had a job. More than likely, she did, unless her husband had left her financially secure. There were so many things he wanted to ask her, but most of them would have to wait until he knew her better.

He could guess at most of the answers, however. If Natalie worked at all, she worked indoors. Her skin was very fair and her hands were soft and perfectly manicured. The diamond and emerald ring on her right hand told him she wasn't hurting for money. But most obvious to him was the shy, almost nervous way she acted whenever he saw her. Either she was unaccustomed to being with men in general, or something about him bothered her. Matt wished he knew the answer to that one.

An hour later, the baseball diamond was dotted with boys of all sizes. Their gloves were ready, their eyes on Bryon as he stepped into the batter's box. Billy, a long-legged, towheaded boy, was pitching. Behind the plate was Casey. His ear-to-ear grin showed through the wires of his catcher's mask.

"Come on, Billy. Fire it in here!" Casey yelled.

And Billy did just that. The hardball whizzed by Bryon and smacked the catcher's mitt long before Bryon's bat swung.

Natalie, who was standing behind the batter's box, shook her head. Bryon looked up at her with eyes that begged for help.

Matt was acting as umpire. As she walked over to the batter's box, she gave him a smile that said they'd both expected this.

"Bryon, I tried to warn you. This isn't five pitch, like you played last year. Billy's not going to lob it over the plate just so you can hit it. He's going to throw it hard. He's trying for strikes."

She repositioned her son's hands on the bat and squared him up to home plate. "Now choke up, keep the bat level, and most of all, don't wait for the ball. When you see it leave his hand, you start to swing, okay?"

Bryon nodded. "I'll try, Mom."

She gave him an encouraging smile. "That's all you have to do to hit it. Okay, Billy. Let it go," she told the pitcher.

Bryon's swing was late again. But at least this time he was close enough to tip the ball. On the fourth pitch Bryon managed to connect with the ball. It fell and rolled just a few feet in front of home plate, but that was enough to send him flying toward first base. Casey tossed aside his mask and lunged for the ball. The runner who had been on first was already halfway to second, but Casey reared back and threw the ball to the second baseman anyway. The throw was high and the boy had to jump to catch it. By the time the dust had settled, the runner had slid safely into the base and Bryon was standing on first with a wide grin.

Behind the plate, Matt was trying to hide his laughter. Natalie looked at Casey, then over at Matt. It was hard to keep a straight face, but somehow she managed. "Would you like to handle this?" she asked Matt, humor edging into her words.

He shook his head. "Oh, no. I'm only the umpire. You're the coach."

"Thanks," she said dryly and faced the catcher.

"Casey," she said as gently as she could, "why did you throw to second base?"

The boy's eyes rounded. "Because, Mrs. Fuller, that was the lead-off man. You always want to get the lead-off man."

She sighed and shook her head. "That's true sometimes, but at other times, you have to sacrifice the lead-off man and take the easy out. Now, instead of Bryon being thrown out at first, both runners are safe. Do you understand?"

Casey nodded glumly, but Natalie didn't let his downtrodden expression put her off. Shading her eyes with her hand, she peered out toward second base. "Okay, Tim, throw the ball back in. Casey's going to try it again."

Casey groaned as the ball flew over his head. Matt stuck his bare hand up and caught it. His reflexes astounded Natalie. She tried not to show her surprise as he gently tossed the ball to Casey.

"You'd better listen to her, son," he said with a confident wink at the boy. "She knows what she's doing."

Casey nodded his head dejectedly. "Yeah, but I don't," he complained.

"You will, though. This is only the second practice. We all have a long way to go."

Matt lifted his vivid blue eyes to Natalie and a strange little tingle ran down the skin between her breasts. Was he talking only about baseball? Her imagination always ran rampant when he was with her, so she couldn't be sure about anything.

With great effort, she pulled herself together. "All right, Tim, Casey. I want you to act like there's a runner heading to second."

Casey wound up and threw the ball with all his might, but he still had it too high and off to the left.

Shaking her head again and walking across the diamond, Natalie called, "Infield, I want every one of you to come in closer. You should see this, too."

Matt started walking toward the boys but Natalie looked his way. "I thought you were the umpire."

He chuckled and moved closer to her. "I like to watch you in action."

She cast him a rueful glance. "Maybe you ought to explain this. They'd probably listen better to you," she said so only he could hear it.

"I think they're listening to you just fine."

"I can see you're going to be fun to work with."

She realized they were ill-chosen words, as his features creased with pure devilry. "I'll remember you said that when you get really mad at me," he told her.

Natalie looked at him in dismay. Did he think they were going to become that close? "I doubt it will happen," she said coolly. "It takes a lot to make me really mad at anyone."

Matt crowed with laughter. "Then, lady, you've never been around anyone like me."

Natalie would have said, "That's for sure," but they had arrived at second base and the boys surrounded them in a tight little circle.

She let out a breath and tried to remember where she was. "Okay, team, when a runner is approaching second, third or home, where are you going to throw the ball? Casey?"

He shrugged and Matt looked at her engagingly. "I know, coach," he said, making many of the boys snicker.

Matt Tanner was, among other things, full of mischief, Natalie thought. "I *know* you do, Matt."

Natalie took Tim's glove from him, jammed it on her left hand and straddled the white bag. "Okay, the runner is headed toward the base. What's he going to be doing, waltzing in?"

The boys giggled. "He'll be sliding in, Mrs. Fuller," one of the older ones answered.

"Right," she said. "And if he's sliding in, how is Tim going to tag him out with his glove up in the sky? Your throw should be on the right side of the bag, almost in the dirt." To illustrate what she was saying, she placed the glove on the ground between her tennis shoe and the base. "That way the runner will slide into it and tag himself out. If your throw is too high, he's going to slide right under it, be called safe and probably go on to score. This doesn't just go for Casey, it means everyone. Got it?"

There were a few yelps and a bit of humming and hawing. For the next twenty minutes they practiced what Natalie had shown them, then continued with the batting. The boys were pretty well worn out by the time dusk arrived and practice was over.

True to his word, Matt had brought the refreshments. As Natalie helped him fill paper cups, she was surprised to find a bag of cookies among the ice.

"You shouldn't have bought these, too," she told him. "The boys only expect something to drink."

"I didn't buy them, Granny made them. She's partial to little boys," he said with a wink.

"That was very kind of her," Natalie said. "Is your grandmother getting on in years?"

"She's seventy, but she acts twenty years younger."

"Sounds like you visit her often."

"Visit her often?" he repeated wryly. "I live with her and Pa."

"Oh, I see," Natalie said, but actually she didn't see at all. She'd heard him mention his granny at the last practice but she never dreamed he lived with his grand-parents. He just didn't seem the type. Most men of his age with his looks would be living in a bachelor pad, freewheeling and free-living. Obviously Matt Tanner wasn't like that.

One of the parents who had been watching the prac-tice approached Natalie as she sat down on the bleachers to enjoy her cold drink.

Although she made polite conversation, Natalie's at-tention was fully on Matt and one of the fathers who'd cornered him down at the opposite end of the bleachers. She kept wishing he'd join her as he'd done last week.

The other woman finally said goodbye. Natalie got up and headed toward the trash barrel to toss away her pa-per cup. Bryon ambled up beside her.

"Mom, I was awful today. I looked like I needed to be back in tee ball."

She put her arm around his shoulders and gave him a little squeeze. "You weren't awful. Everyone has to learn. The thirteen-year-olds went through the same transition you're going through now," she assured him.

"Maybe," he said, looking dejected. "But I don't know if I'll ever be able to hit a ball pitched that fast."

She laughed softly. "Oh, yes you will, honey. You'll be able to hit and Casey will be able to throw. Danny will be able to catch a foul ball, and so on and so forth. By the time the games start, everyone will be doing just fine. You'll see."

Bryon gave her a small smile. "Aw, Mom, you always make everything sound so simple."

"That's what moms are for. Didn't you know that?" She dropped her arm from his shoulder. "So, are you ready to go home now?"

"Can't we talk to Mr. Tanner first?"

Natalie looked down the bleachers. Matt was still deep in conversation with Tim Birney's dad. She felt a ridiculous pang of disappointment.

"Mr. Tanner is busy." Besides, she told herself, he'd just spent the past two hours with her and the boys out on the field.

Natalie and Bryon were in the car and she was backing out toward the highway when Matt came trotting over to them.

"Why are you leaving so early?" he asked. "I thought we might talk about the team for a few minutes."

Her heart was racing as she leaned out the window and looked up at him. "It's late. I need to get Bryon some dinner." Louise was probably watching the house now, wondering why they hadn't made it home. Natalie frowned to herself. It was a dismal thought.

"Why don't I take you and Bryon out for a hamburger? I haven't eaten yet, either."

"Can we, Mom?" Bryon asked, bouncing up and down on the edge of the seat.

Natalie would have liked nothing better than to spend a bit more time with this man, but, on the other hand, she would be asking for trouble if she did. Probably people she knew would see them and the gossip would start. Fort Gibson was a small place—one of the leading pastimes was tongue-wagging, and she couldn't let Bryon or herself be the subject of rumor.

"I planned to make pizza at home," she said, "thanks anyway."

Bryon looked crestfallen for an instant, then his face lit up with an idea, "Mr. Tanner, why don't you come over and have pizza with us? Mom always makes a big one."

Natalie struggled to keep from chiding Bryon and withdrawing his offer.

"I'm sure she does," Matt said. "But an invitation like that would have to come from your mom."

Would he actually accept? she wondered with a hint of desperation. She'd never invited a man to her house before. Louise would be livid. But that little voice that seemed to want to take her over said, "So what." Why should Louise object to her having a man eat pizza in her kitchen? There was nothing immoral in that, was there?

"We'd be happy to share our pizza," she said, venturing to glance up at him. "That is, if you don't mind taking a chance on my cooking."

Natalie couldn't ignore the sudden sparkle in his eye. She felt breathless when he said, "Just let me get my truck and I'll follow you."

Chapter Four

Y̶ou have a very nice place," Matt said as he joined Natalie on the concrete drive in front of her house.

Bryon had already shot up the steps and through the door, leaving the adults to follow at a slower pace. Natalie had to restrain herself from glancing across the fence at her in-laws' house. Without looking, she knew Louise was peering through the drapes. In five minutes, the phone would be ringing.

"Thank you," she told him. "It's been my home for a long time."

She unlocked the door and held it for him. Once inside, he took off his baseball cap and Natalie hung it on the hall tree.

Matt watched her walk across the room. It wasn't the first time he had noticed how gently and gracefully she moved. Watching her both soothed and disturbed him.

The room was elegant, but it had a warm, lived-in charm. Obviously the place meant a lot to her. Matt liked that—the only thing about Natalie that he *didn't* like was that she didn't belong to him.

A year or two ago, that discovery would have probably put him in a panic, but not now. Funny, how confident he felt, now that he'd found the right woman.

"This room reminds me of you," he commented.

She looked at him with surprise. "Really? I never thought about it."

Matt nodded toward the old upright piano standing in one corner. "Do you play?"

"A little. I fill in at church when the regular pianist is away. But that's about all."

Bryon could be heard thumping down the hall just before he burst into the room. Water dripped from his hair. He'd hastily washed his face and hands.

"Mr. Tanner, would you like to see my new ten-speed? I got it for my birthday."

"Bryon, Matt just walked in the door. Don't you think he needs to catch his breath?"

Her son shrugged. "He looks all right to me."

Natalie rolled her eyes and Matt chuckled. "Sure, I'd like to see it, Bryon. Just lead the way."

As the two of them started to head for the patio doors, the telephone rang. Natalie knew who it was. She stared at the phone with helpless frustration, but Bryon saved her by lifting the receiver.

"Oh, hi, Grandma. Yes, it's over with. No. Mom's going to fix pizza. Oh, him, that's my coach. I gotta go now, Grandma. Bye." Bryon hung up the phone.

At any other time, Natalie would have chastised her son for cutting his grandmother short, but not now. Louise had only been pumping Bryon for information.

"You two go ahead," she told Matt and her son. "I'll be fixing the pizza."

From the kitchen, Natalie listened to the murmur of their voices through the window screens. She marveled at the endless stream of talk coming from Bryon. He was usually a quiet boy, even with his best friend. There must be something about Matt he respected and trusted. She hoped that wasn't a bad thing, for Bryon's sake *and* for her sake.

The pizza was almost ready for the oven when they came into the living room. Natalie was amazed to see Matt joining her in the kitchen.

"That looks delicious," he said, eyeing the pizza.

"Thank you," she said self-consciously. "I hope it tastes delicious, too."

"Don't worry," Bryon said, sitting atop a bar stool. "Everything Mom makes is good. The only thing she can't cook is divinity candy. It comes out like gooey white glue."

"Thanks, Bryon," she joked.

Matt chuckled. "We all have our shortcomings. Mine is cooking in general. Scrambled eggs and toast is about as far as I go."

"Yuck! I'd get pretty tired of that," Bryon said.

"I did. That's why I ate at restaurants and fast-food places while I was rodeoing. Now I have Granny's cooking."

"Can she cook well?" Bryon wanted to know.

Matt smiled. "About as well as your mother, I'd say."

Natalie blushed. "I really doubt I'm as good a cook as she is," she said, feeling the kitchen shrink around her. Every time she looked at Matt she was mesmerized by the way his muscles flexed in his arms, by the set of his shoulders, the sun streaks of blonde in his hair and the sizzling blue of his eyes. She felt guilty, as if looking was a sinful thing to do. It *was* sinful, she supposed, to look at him the way she was looking. She prayed that Matt couldn't read anything in her eyes.

"Why don't you have a seat at the bar?" she offered. "I'll get you something to drink. I don't have any beer, but there are some wine coolers. Would you like one?"

"Sounds good to me," he said, taking a seat at the counter that divided the kitchen from the dining area.

Natalie got a cooler from the refrigerator, then started to open a cabinet and take down a glass.

"Don't waste that on me," Matt said, stopping her. "I'm not that refined."

She smiled and crossed the kitchen to hand him the frosty bottle. As he took it, his fingers inadvertently brushed hers. His hand was rough. It was as if an electrical current ran from it and into her bloodstream.

After a moment, she asked, "Are you sure you don't want a glass?"

Matt shook his head. His eyes crinkled at the corners as he smiled at her. "I should work my way up to it, don't you think?"

She looked at him blankly. "Work up to what?"

"Being more refined."

"Refinement is for people who want to make a certain impression. Somehow, I don't believe you have the need to do that."

His eyes sparkled as a slow grin spread over his mouth. "You got that right. But—" he shrugged and took a sip of the cooler. "There's always room for a person to better himself."

"I agree. But I don't believe in changing yourself just to please someone else." Then Natalie realized all the changes she'd made in herself to conform to James's way of living. Of course, some had only been minor things that naturally came about when two people are learning to share. But many other changes had not been so minor. She'd given up several of her ideals and pleasures in order to make James happy. She'd never do that again.

Matt eyed her curiously as she walked across to the refrigerator. "You sound awfully sure about that."

"I am."

"Mom, can we eat out on the patio?" Bryon asked eagerly. "It's warm tonight."

Natalie got lettuce and tomatoes out of the vegetable bin. "Okay, if you'll carry out all the things and set the table," she told her son.

The boy slid from his seat next to Matt and quickly went to work gathering plates and silverware.

As Matt watched mother and son bustle around the kitchen, he wondered if Natalie had ever changed for someone. Was it her husband? He couldn't imagine that. Why would anyone want her to change? He loved her exactly the way she was. Love? Matt took a deep breath, closed his eyes and swallowed nearly half of his drink.

Thirty minutes later, the three of them had downed a bowl of salad and more than half the pizza. The night was warm and pleasant, as Bryon had said. Natalie leaned back in her wicker chair and sighed contentedly.

The back of the house was built in an L-shape. Locally quarried rock had been laid in the corner to create the patio. To their left, redwood latticework covered with dense ivy shielded them from the neighbors. This was Natalie's favorite spot to relax in the spring and summer. She was glad to be sharing it with Matt tonight. From the look on her son's face, he thought so, too.

"So, how does it feel to be off the road and living with your grandparents?" she asked.

Matt rested his forearms against the glass tabletop and gazed at Natalie. "Not as strange as you might think.

Actually, it feels like finally coming home. You see, I've lived with Pa and Granny for eighteen years—ever since I was ten."

He was twenty-eight! She was five years older than him. She struggled to keep the shock out of her expression. "Oh," she said, exhaling a long breath. "Are your parents dead?"

He shook his head. "Divorced. But I lived with Pa and Granny even before then. My parents didn't always provide the ideal environment for a child, if you know what I mean. I was better off here in Oklahoma."

Natalie's eyes moved from Matt's rueful expression to her son's. She could see Bryon was all ears and she supposed Matt was reluctant to elaborate on the subject. Too bad, she thought. Bryon was not the only curious one. More and more, she wanted to know everything about this man.

Suddenly the telephone rang. Bryon jumped up to answer it. A few moments later, he burst through the door and onto the patio.

"Mom, Jimmy's family is making homemade ice cream! They want me to come over and eat some. Can I? I mean, may I?"

"I don't know, Bryon. It's getting late. Besides, I've made dessert, too."

"You and Matt can eat it," he reasoned.

"That's another thing," she said firmly. "We have company and—"

"Hey, wait a minute," Matt interrupted. "I don't want Bryon to miss ice cream on my account. You can't count *me* as his company—I'm just his coach."

"See, Mom? Matt doesn't care."

Natalie let out a resigned sigh. "Okay, you can go. But have Shirley drive you home. I don't want you walking back late, even if it is only three blocks."

"I will. Thanks, Mom!" He gave her a quick hug around the neck then raced past the house and out of sight.

"You know, I believe you remember clearly how it was to be his age," she said teasingly to Matt.

His smile was a little sheepish. "Well, you don't forget things like that. What about you? What do you most remember about being Bryon's age?" he asked lazily.

Natalie reached for her soft drink. "Actually, most of my memories are of moving. My father was—and still is—in the army. I'd gone through several schools by the time I was eleven."

"I know what you mean. I jumped from place to place a lot, too—until Granny and Pa took me in."

A nostalgic smile tilted Natalie's lips. "What I remember most about moving so much was the first day in a new school. The teacher would say 'Class, we've got a new student today,' and about thirty pairs of eyes would look at you as if you'd just landed from Mars."

Matt chuckled. "I remember that feeling. And just when you'd found the very best friend you ever had, you'd come home and your parents would say it was time to move again."

Natalie groaned. "Oh, don't remind me. I cried for a week because I had to leave one of my friends. Judy was her name. We were thirteen and thought every boy in junior high was in love with us."

"Maybe they were," he said with a coy grin.

"I doubt it. I had braces and freckles then, and Judy's skin was a mess."

Matt laughed heartily and Natalie found herself joining him. She'd often looked back with regret on her little childhood miseries. It was nice to find she could share them with someone.

"It's amazing how everything seems so important and intense when you're that age," Matt mused.

Natalie nodded. She reached for an olive on her plate. "That's just what I was thinking."

As she popped the olive into her mouth she felt Matt studying her. "Do you know what I'm thinking?" he asked softly.

She lifted her eyes to his. "What?"

"That I'm very glad Leonard talked me into this baseball thing. Otherwise I might never have met you."

Her throat suddenly tightened around the olive. Natalie swallowed convulsively and glanced away from him.

"I am, too," she said, coughing to camouflage the quiver in her voice. "Otherwise I might have been stuck with Dan Jenkins again."

Before he could say anything else she rose to her feet. "Are you ready for dessert?"

"Sure."

Without looking at him, she hurried into the house. But just as she bent to pull parfait glasses from the refrigerator, Matt's footsteps sounded on the tile floor.

"I don't know who this Dan Jenkins is, but I wanted to hear you say you were glad just because it was me."

Natalie turned to face him. He was standing only a few inches from her and she was suddenly aware of a panicky breathlessness attacking her lungs. "Look, Matt, I—I just—"

His serious expression quickly turned to a frown. "I know," he said softly. "You don't have to tell me. You don't want to get involved."

Her green eyes widened in astonishment, but he continued, "Natalie, you have that cool, untouched look about you."

Her lips twisted with irony. "That sounds a little ridiculous, doesn't it? After all, I do have a son."

He took a step forward and Natalie involuntarily retreated until her back was brushing the cool door of the refrigerator. When he reached out his right hand and planted it by her head, she felt trapped, yet strangely reluctant to escape.

"Bryon is eleven years old. And how long has your husband been dead?"

In spite of the chaotic things she was thinking, she met his eyes. "Eight years."

"That's a long time."

Natalie swallowed as the warm, male scent of him filled her senses. She imagined how it would feel to be in his arms. Warm, intoxicating and wonderful. He could make a woman forget where she was, forget who she was—and he was only inches away from her. It would be so easy, but she couldn't let that happen!

Abruptly, she ducked under his arm and walked as sedately as possible to the bar. She placed the parfait glasses on the counter, taking a deep breath and trying to get hold of herself.

Without warning, his fingers closed around her upper arm. Natalie flinched at his touch. "I want to know you better, Natalie."

He pulled her around to face him. "Then you have your wants and your needs mixed up," she told him.

Hurt flared faintly in the blue gleam of his eyes—and turned to anger. "What do you know about my wants *or* needs?" he demanded.

Her gaze fell from his face and fixed itself on the buttons of her blouse. She could almost see them moving as her heart pounded heavily in her breast. *I'm not equipped for this,* she thought fearfully. James had been easy to deal with even when she'd been young and immature—he'd always kept his composure. But this man was excitement and passion, a man of action, not words. It was written all over him. She'd never dealt with anyone like him before. "I know what most men think about widows and divorcées."

"Really?" he said tightly. "Maybe you'd better let me in on it. Pa wouldn't want me going around being uninformed about women. Not after he's done his best to teach me about them for the last fifteen years."

Resentment burned inside her. He was goading her to admit something that he already knew. "You know what I'm talking about," she said tartly. "We're supposed to be love-starved, easy prey."

Matt shook his head in disbelief. He muttered an oath just under his breath. "Is that what you think? That I'm some guy on the prowl looking for a roll in the hay? I'm not that desperate for a social life."

Natalie winced at his frankness, but the anger inside her made her brave. She brought her gaze up to meet his. "I don't know what you think! I don't know *you*. And you don't know me! For your information, this is the first time I've invited a man to this house since James died. I should have known better!"

Matt couldn't believe the power this woman had over him. He'd thought he could laugh anything off, but she—she made him so damn angry! "What is that supposed to mean? I'm not guilty of anything except admitting that I'd like to know you better. Is that a crime?"

Natalie looked down at his tanned fingers, still clenched tightly around her arm. They were strong and sensual—so different from her own white skin pressed beneath their grasp. That very difference was what made his touch so appealing. "Yes," she answered. "It's a crime to me. I don't get involved. You're right. No dates, no affairs, no nothing."

She sounded so cold and unaffected that he had to fight the urge to shake her. "Why? Are you still in love with your husband?"

In the next instant, Natalie's palm slapped against his jaw. Yet before she could feel any satisfaction from the blow, Matt had jerked her against him.

Natalie struggled for a moment, then his mouth fastened on hers and she forgot they'd been fighting. The touch of his lips was electric, fusing her to him with white-hot fire. She couldn't pull away, not when the hungry search of his mouth was giving her body everything it craved, not when the hands around her waist were drawing her closer and closer to the warm, delicious feel of him.

In the end, it was Matt who ended the kiss. They were both breathing hard. His eyes smoldered. "I'm not asking you to go to bed with me, Natalie. I'm just asking you to share some of your time, to get to know me. Let me get to know you," he murmured in a warm, husky voice.

Natalie had the strongest urge to cry. Tears ached in her throat as she whispered, "It won't work, Matt. You'd be wasting your time."

"Why?" he persisted.

She blinked, hoping the moisture in her eyes didn't spill out and embarrass her. "Oh, you must be either blind or a glutton for punishment. I'm older than you, Matt."

He looked completely befuddled. "So? That just means you've had more time to grow beautiful. And you are beautiful, Natalie. Very beautiful."

The sensuous tone of his voice alerted her senses to danger. With all the effort she could muster, she pulled away from him and reached for the parfait glasses. The last thing she wanted now was to eat, but she had to do something to end this insanity.

"I think we'd better go back outside and eat our dessert. Bryon will be back soon."

"I'll be gone by then," he assured her as he accepted the glass she offered him. "But this is only the beginning for us, Natalie."

She clenched her fingers around the cold glass and met his determined gaze. *I won't argue with him,* Natalie thought. *I'll just prove to him that I can never lay my heart open for him or any other man, ever again.*

"Is anything wrong, Natalie? You've been awfully quiet today. Half of your lunch is still on your plate."

Natalie put down her plastic fork and looked across the table at her friend Dana. The two of them had walked down the mall to eat at a fast-food restaurant during their lunch break.

"I'm not hungry," Natalie said, pushing away the now soggy salad.

"You've been staring into space for the past fifteen minutes. You don't even know what's on your plate. What's wrong? Are you ill? Mrs. Greer will let you have the rest of the afternoon off."

Natalie shook her head. "No. I'm not ill. I'm just not with it today. I didn't sleep very well last night." That was an understatement, Natalie thought. She had slept a total of two hours, spending the rest of the night tossing

back and forth. She couldn't get Matt out of her mind—
the things he'd said to her, the way he'd looked, and,
most of all, the way his kiss had stirred her.

She was headed for trouble. Today all she'd done was
try to decide what to do about him. Should she resign as
coach and let Matt handle it by himself? It was a cow-
ardly thing to do, but Natalie was in such a state, she
didn't know if she could handle seeing him that often.
But there was Bryon to consider. He wouldn't understand her quitting. How could he? Not even Natalie
understood her almost instant attraction to Matt Tanner. She certainly couldn't let her son know about it.
He'd never had to consider the idea of a new man in their
lives. What would it do to him?

Dana's voice penetrated her thoughts and with a guilty
start, Natalie realized she hadn't been listening to her
friend.

"I'm sorry, Dana, what were you saying?"

Frowning, the blond woman studied Natalie. "I asked
if everything went all right with the baseball team last
night. I know you've been excited about it starting this
spring."

Baseball. Sometimes Natalie wished she'd never heard
of it. But that was a silly attitude, she chided herself.
Baseball had nothing to do with love. *Love.* Was that
what was happening to her? Falling in love with someone she barely knew—the idea was more than frighten-
ing.

"Yes. Practice went fine," Natalie finally answered.

"How do you like the guy who's helping you? What's
he like?"

Dana didn't realize she had struck a nerve, and Natalie didn't want her to know it, either. "He's very nice,"
she answered sincerely. "Very good with the boys."

Dana downed the last of her soft drink and pulled a compact and a tube of lipstick from her purse. Natalie watched as she spread the pink color over her lips. "Is he married or single?"

Natalie frowned. "What does that have to do with anything?"

"Just curious." Dana shrugged, putting away her makeup.

"Does David know you're curious about other men?"

Dana looked at her friend and burst out laughing. "Silly, I've got a husband. I was asking for your sake."

Natalie was flabbergasted. "*My* sake! When did you decide I need a husband?"

Dana's blue eyes clouded thoughtfully. "Hmm. I'd say about two and a half years ago—a month after I got to know you."

Natalie pushed a piece of wilted lettuce across the Styrofoam plate with her fork. Dana had often suggested that Natalie start dating, but she'd never mentioned marriage before. Dana was only twenty-five, had been happily married for four years and had a two-year-old daughter. She believed everyone could be as happy as she was. Dana was a confirmed romantic.

"Look, Dana, I know you mean well, but I've already been married. I know what it's like."

"Is that all you can say?" Dana asked in dismay. "My word, Natalie, you're young and beautiful. Your life could be so full."

"My life *is* full," Natalie argued.

Dana groaned. "Natalie, from what you've told me, your marriage to James was a happy one."

"Yes. I loved him, he loved me. We had a child, a home and all the trimmings."

"Wouldn't you like to have it again?"

"No!"

"Why? Are you afraid you'd lose it all again?"

Natalie suddenly remembered the cold, icy night the police knocked on her door, the terrible black pain she'd felt when they told her James was dead. No one should go through that kind of grief twice.

"Maybe," she conceded. "But that's not the only reason."

"Then what is it?" Dana said.

Natalie rose and picked up her purse. How did they get started on this subject anyway, she wondered irritably. "Believe me, there are a lot of reasons. Now hurry up, or we'll be late getting back to work."

Dana cast her a taunting look. She must think I'm a coward, Natalie thought, but she didn't care. She just wished she could forget all about Matt Tanner.

"You never did answer my question, you know," Dana said as they left the restaurant and began walking down the crowded mall.

"What question?"

"The coach. Is he single or married?"

Natalie pretended to be very interested in the window displays they were passing. "Single."

Dana's young face developed a knowing little smile, but Natalie missed it. "Is he good-looking?"

"Very."

"Do you like him?"

Natalie glanced at Dana. "Yes. I do like him," she admitted with dawning realization. True, he was young, he oozed masculinity and he'd led an exciting life—far different from hers. But he'd set high standards for himself. Natalie especially liked that—and the sensitivity he showed to others. "I like him very much."

Chapter Five

"Then what's the problem?" Dana asked.

Natalie sighed. Why was Dana doing this today, of all days? "There's no problem, Dana. I don't know why you think there is."

Dana shook her head as she skirted around a woman pushing a baby buggy. "Because, my dear friend, I've never seen you acting this way. You've always been on top of everything, but I doubt you heard half of what the customers asked for today."

Natalie grimaced. "Oh, dear, I was afraid my work wasn't up to snuff today."

"Natalie, that's not the point. You know—" She broke off as she noticed the miserable expression on her friend's face. "Okay, I won't hound you anymore. I just want you to know I'm here if you need me."

"Thanks. You're a sweet friend." She glanced at her watch. "We've got two minutes to spare. Jerry can't find fault with us today."

The store was crowded with noon-hour shoppers. Poor Jerry had left the men's department to cover for Natalie. With a desperate look on his face, he beckoned to her.

"Thank God you're here; this was about to get embarrassing," he whispered in her ear. She noticed an elderly female customer standing by him.

Natalie had to stifle a smile as Jerry said, full-voice, "Natalie, this lady would like to purchase a girdle. Could you help her out?"

Turning to the woman, she said politely, "Of course. Let me show you what we have in stock."

It took a good ten minutes for the customer to finally choose a girdle she liked. The whole time, Dana kept waving at Natalie from the checkout counter several feet away. What was she trying to tell her? What had put that silly-looking grin on her friend's face?

After the customer left with her purchase, Natalie approached Dana, who reached under the counter and pulled out some yellow roses. They had obviously just been delivered from the florist. The card was still pinned to the green fern nestled against the long-stemmed roses.

"Oh, no wonder, you've got that dreamy look on your face. David sent you flowers. What's the occasion?"

Dana's blue eyes twinkled merrily. "You tell me. It's for you."

"What?" Natalie cried. She grabbed the crystal-cut vase Dana was thrusting at her.

"You heard me. Now hurry and open the card!"

Setting the vase down on the countertop, Natalie unpinned the small envelope from the greenery. Questions raced through her head as she fumbled with the card.

Natalie flushed as she read: *You said I didn't need to try to make an impression. But I do need to apologize to you for being so insensitive last night. Can you forgive an uncouth cowboy? Matt.*

She exhaled shakily as she hurriedly jammed the card into the envelope. Feeling Dana's stare, she sniffed the lovely roses. Yellow was her favorite color. Funny that he'd chosen to send her roses just that shade.

"Well," Dana said impatiently, "are you going to tell me who sent it?"

Natalie's mind was suddenly racing. Matt had meant what he'd told her last night. What was she going to do? How could she hide now? Dana was waiting for an answer. She couldn't lie to her. Nothing like this had ever happened to her before. She'd never *allowed* it to happen, Natalie corrected, but then she'd never met anyone like Matthew Tanner before.

"It's from Matt. The man you were asking me about."

Dana's face burst into a wide grin. Natalie turned away from her with sudden frustration. "Dana, don't look at me that way! There's nothing going on between us."

Natalie shoved the card into her purse. She looked up to see Dana's incredulous expression.

"Why not?"

A slightly hysterical laugh bubbled out of Natalie's throat. "Don't be insane. I'm too old for romance. I put it out of my life years ago."

Dana's eyes widened. "Don't be such an idiot, Natalie. Age has nothing to do with love."

"You're only seeing things through young eyes. I've already had as much love and romance as I'll ever need," Natalie said, trying to sound convincing.

A gentleman with an armload of slacks and shirts was approaching the checkout counter, but before he reached them, Dana leaned down and hissed in Natalie's ear, "You can never have enough love and romance."

Natalie gave her an impatient glare and said, "Please check him out, will you? I'm going to hang out the new bathing suits."

Dana nodded and Natalie started around the edge of the counter. As she passed, she took a quick glance at the roses once more. In spite of all her protests, Natalie felt flattered and deeply happy that Matt had done such an unexpected, sentimental thing. James had sent her flowers for traditional times like her birthday or anniversary, but never out of the blue. James had been a relatively predictable man, but Matt Tanner was the furthest thing from predictable that Natalie could imagine.

As Natalie hung scanty bikinis and sleek, colorful maillots on a rack, Jerry ambled over and leaned casually against a counter of printed T-shirts.

He was thirty years old, a bachelor and a firm believer in partying at least three nights a week. Jerry was full of nonsense, but he was a pleasant person to work with— he'd often gone out of his way to cover her area when she'd needed to leave early.

"Thanks for coming to the rescue. I'm not acquainted with girdles."

She gave him a wry grin. "I hope not."

He nodded toward the rack of bathing suits. "You going to buy yourself one of those?"

Natalie laughed teasingly. "Sure. Can't you just see me in one of these things?"

Jerry's dark gaze slid over her petite form. "Why not? I bet you'd get some whistles."

She arched her fine brows with disdain. "I wouldn't want any whistles."

"Natalie—" Jerry chuckled "—you are the most prim and proper woman I've ever met."

"I'm not prim. I'm just a sensible adult and mother."

"I'll excuse you for that."

She slanted a look of annoyance at him. "Don't you have anybody to wait on?"

He pushed himself away from the counter. "No, let me show you what I mean. You know I'm great with fashion."

He reached for the button at her collar. "You need to undo this, let a little skin show."

The button popped loose and Jerry pulled the lapels of her blouse out toward her shoulders. Natalie slapped his hands away, but he laughed and reached for the folds of her loose skirt. "Now, I'd say you need to hem this up to about right here."

He'd pulled her skirt a good three inches higher than it was. She whirled away from him. "Cut that out. I have more important things to worry about and I like my clothes the way they are."

He laughed and, having obviously decided he'd pestered her long enough, began to stroll back to the men's area. "Well, you're doing the world a great disservice by covering up all that beauty."

Natalie groaned and went back to the bathing suits. She knew Jerry and those wild parties he went to, and she knew he'd probably done more than just rearrange a woman's clothing. He was an outrageous flirt and changed girlfriends at least every four to six weeks. Despite his wild life-style, he always seemed to go out with attractive women.

Looking closer at the bathing suits, she thought about Jerry's words. Did she really look good enough to wear one of these things? She pulled a bright yellow and white bikini from the rack and held it in front of her. It was scandalously skimpy and she laughed to imagine the look on Louise's face if she ever saw Natalie wearing such a thing in the backyard.

She hung it back on the metal rod and lifted out a one-piece suit shaded in aqua, turquoise and white. The colors were beautiful. She fingered it thoughtfully. It really wasn't all *that* revealing, she told herself. The front would show a bit of cleavage, but after all, it was a bathing suit. You were supposed to expose a little bit on the beach, weren't you?

Realizing what she was about to do, Natalie swiftly hung the suit back on the rod. *No,* she told herself firmly. *Your old black suit is fine for taking Bryon to the lake. Just because a man sends you roses doesn't mean you should go out and buy yourself some daring new fashion.*

But you are young, said a little voice inside her. *Thirty-three isn't old, is it?* Even if Natalie wasn't quite what she'd call beautiful, she wasn't all that bad, either. Her hair was pretty. Everyone said so.

She approached one of the three-way mirrors and studied her image. Her skin was still smooth and her mouth was pretty when she wore lipstick.

You're very beautiful, Natalie. Matt's low masculine voice rang in her memory.

Did he really think so? What could he possibly see in her? She was five years older than he was. Plenty of women would be interested in him, but he wanted her. The idea was both exhilarating and embarrassing to Natalie. Lord, what would Louise think if she knew?

Stop it, she ordered the voice in her head. *No one will ever think anything, because you're not going to let it go that far.*

But his kiss was still warm and fresh in her memory. To think of never experiencing it again was like looking into a black pit.

Suddenly decisive Natalie walked back to the bathing suits and pulled the aqua suit off the hanger. When she took it over to the checkout counter, she felt as if she'd taken a step onto new, exciting ground. The feeling was refreshingly good.

Louise was in the kitchen with Bryon when Natalie arrived home that evening. She eyed the roses and the package in Natalie's arms suspiciously.

"Hi, Mom," Bryon said.

"Hi, darling. Hello, Louise."

"Pretty roses. Who gave you them, dear?" her mother-in-law asked.

Louise made getting sent flowers sound like a crime—she'd certainly think it was, if she'd known who sent them.

"Hey, Mom! I got a hundred and four on my spelling test today!"

Bryon's interruption was a godsend. It rescued her from answering Louise.

"Really? How'd you manage that?" she asked as she crossed the room. Natalie placed the roses in the middle of the oak dining table and she turned toward Bryon's beaming face.

"I got two bonus words right and I hadn't even studied them! Did you buy me something?"

He sidled up to her and tried to peer inside the package jammed beneath her arm. Natalie laughed and tweaked his nose.

"No, I bought myself something this time. Some clothing, that's all."

"Oh? Let's see it," Louise said.

Natalie looked at her mother-in-law, who had perched on one of the bar stools. She'd made herself quite at home. There was a glass of iced tea in front of her and a plate of cookies Natalie had made the night before. Natalie thought it was a little ungrateful of her, but she definitely resented Louise's assumption that she had free run of the house. It wasn't the food she ate or the snooping that bothered Natalie. It was being taken for granted. Louise seemed to think that whatever belonged to Natalie, belonged to her, too—Bryon, especially.

Bryon slid the sack from beneath his mother's arm and pulled out the colorful bathing suit. "Wow! That's pretty, Mom! When you gonna wear it?"

She smiled at her son. "Whenever we go to the lake, as soon as the water warms up."

Louise made a little humph of outrage. "You don't plan on wearing that in *public*, do you?"

Natalie patiently closed her eyes. She neatly folded the bathing suit and placed it back in the sack. "I wouldn't have paid a day's wages for it if I didn't plan to wear it."

"Natalie, I would never have believed it of you!"

"It's only a bathing suit, Louise." Natalie sighed.

"That's right, and there's nothing to it! One of those French-cut things, isn't it? I could tell when Bryon held it up."

"That's the style now," Natalie said, wondering why she bothered trying to explain. Louise always made up her narrow mind long before Natalie could say a word.

"It's not the style for a woman in her thirties with a son nearly twelve years old! What will people think?"

"I think she'll look real foxy." Bryon suddenly spoke up.

Natalie struggled not to smile as Louise's mouth fell open. "And what do you know about it, Bryon? You're only a child."

The boy drew up his shoulders. "I know about that kind of stuff. Mom's pretty. A lot prettier than most of the moms I know."

Louise sputtered, "Well, yes—she is pretty, but—"

Natalie took a deep breath and looked at her son. "Bryon, why don't you go wash up and change your shirt? I've decided to drive over to Muskogee for dinner."

"Gee, great!" Bryon said, already running to the bathroom.

Louise slid from the bar stool. "You know, you two could eat with me and Harvey. I've made goulash."

"That's kind of you, Louise, but I'm in the mood for some seafood." *And the last thing I want to do is spend the evening listening to what happened on the game shows today,* Natalie thought.

Louise ambled toward the door, then turned back to Natalie. "You had a visitor last night."

It sounded like an accusation. "Yes, I did. That was the man who helps me coach the baseball team."

Louise looked at her as if she expected to hear an explanation, but Natalie said nothing. Finally, the older woman said, "He stayed quite late."

Natalie wondered if Louise knew how she was giving her spying away. She doubted it. Louise probably considered it her right to keep tabs on her.

"Not really," Natalie said. "He left before Bryon's bedtime." *But not before we'd made wild, passionate love on the kitchen floor,* she felt like adding.

"I know I shouldn't be saying this, Natalie, but I hope you're not planning on—" Her hands fluttered as she groped for words. "Well, surely your love for James hasn't died this quickly.

Died this quickly, Natalie repeated to herself. Did Louise think eight years went quickly? "My love for James," Natalie echoed with frustration. "What has that got to do with having a guest over?"

Louise sniffed and drew her shoulders up stiffly. "All right, Natalie, if you want me to be frank, I will. I can't believe you are one of those women who puts her husband in the past and goes on to marry another man. There is only one mate given to us on this earth. And we both know James was yours."

Fury swept through Natalie like a blast from a furnace. Louise had said and done many questionable things in the past, but this was incredible!

"Louise, I really think you've drawn the wrong conclusion about this whole thing. Matt is my friend. We work together. It's as simple as that."

Louise sniffed again and darted her a pointed look. "You've never invited any other men over here. There must be something different about this one."

"There is something different," Natalie said, surprising herself and shocking Louise. "He's considerate and funny. I enjoy talking to him."

Louise seemed to be struggling with tears but Natalie knew her actions were pure pretense. It was easy to see the hard, angry glint in her eyes.

"If only poor James were here now," she lamented.

For years Louise had used this tactic to steer Natalie toward her way of thinking—and for years it had worked. Natalie would always feel guilty and ashamed at having upset her mother-in-law. She'd tell herself Louise had lost her only son and the least Natalie could do was to let Louise have her way, to try to get along.

To get along, Natalie thought now with frustration. She'd submitted to Louise in every way imaginable. For the past two or three years, Natalie realized, she'd caused much of the problem herself. If she hadn't been so soft-hearted, if she'd shown a little more decisiveness and determination along the way, Louise wouldn't be thinking she had the right to run Natalie's life.

"James has been gone for a long time, Louise." Natalie sighed. "He isn't here to fill my life anymore."

Louise dropped her fingers from her cheeks and stared at Natalie as if she'd gone mad. "But he lives in our hearts! That's what keeps me going from day to day, knowing that his memory is still fresh and alive in my heart. He's still in yours, too, Natalie. You just don't—"

The thud of Bryon's footsteps halted her words. Natalie was grateful. If he'd come any later, she might have said something she'd regret deeply later.

"Ready, Mom!" Bryon burst through the doorway. He looked from Natalie to his grandmother and the grin faded from his face. "Is something wrong?"

Natalie quickly smiled. "No, nothing's wrong. Your grandmother and I were only talking." She glanced at her mother-in-law. "If you'll excuse me now, Louise, I'm going to freshen up. Bryon," she said, turning to her son, "I'll only be a few minutes."

As Natalie left the room and hurried down the hallway, the slam of the door told her Louise had gone home. She breathed a sigh of great relief.

Ten minutes later, when she and Bryon were driving near the outskirts of Muskogee, he suddenly spoke.

"Mom, you never did say where you got the roses. Did you buy them?"

Natalie glanced across the seat to her son. The look on his young face wasn't suspicious, merely thoughtful. Children must have emotional radar, she thought.

Natalie had never lied to her son, and she didn't intend to start now. "No, I didn't buy them. Matt sent them to me."

Bryon looked at his mother with new eyes. "Really? What'd he do that for?"

One corner of Natalie's mouth lifted. "I suppose because he likes me."

His brown eyes widened as comprehension crept over his face. "You mean he likes you, like a man likes a woman?"

She nodded, wondering what Bryon thought of that. "Yes, that's what I mean. Does it upset you?" she asked carefully.

His face crinkled with confusion. "Shoot, no! I like Matt. I think he's great!"

A smile lit Natalie's face. She hadn't known what to expect from Bryon. Maybe subconsciously she'd expected him to react with outrage and selfishness as his grandmother had.

As she slowed the car at an intersection, her spirits soared. Matt was just a friend, but it was good to know that Bryon would not resent sharing their life with a man if the time came.

Natalie had never planned to become involved with another man. But lately new thoughts came to her. The major part of her life was still ahead of her. Was she going to spend it alone? When old age came there would be no one with whom she could share fond memories, no one to hold her hand and let her know she was still loved. It was a bleak picture.

Louise might be able to live on memories, but Natalie was beginning to realize she couldn't. Memories couldn't keep you warm, they couldn't smile at you, talk to you, kiss you or hold you when you felt empty and alone.

Are you still in love with your husband? Matt had asked. The question had seemed irreverent at the time. Natalie cringed as she recalled how furiously she'd slapped him. But at least the question had jolted her. She knew with a measure of certainty that she wasn't in love with James any longer. Her love for him had died along with her grief—it was all part of letting go.

Natalie smiled again, reached over and ruffled Bryon's hair. "You're a good kid, you know that?"

At the praise, Bryon grinned self-consciously. "You're pretty neat, too, Mom."

It rained all day Friday. Natalie stared out at the gloomy skies as she drove home from work.

There was no sign of change in the weather and disappointment swept over her. They couldn't practice baseball in this. And without the practices, she wouldn't see Matt.

She had thought of him continually since receiving the roses. Natalie had to admit that she missed him. Whether good or bad, he brought a difference, a spark to her life.

Later, she entered the house to hear the telephone ringing. Shaking the water from her dark red hair, she hurried to answer it.

"Hello."

"Natalie, it's me, Matt. How are you?"

Warmth rushed over her at the sound of his voice.

"I'm fine, Matt. Wet, but fine. And you?"

"Getting cabin fever," he answered. "I think I've watched the rain from every window in the house. Looks like it'll be impossible to have practice this evening."

"Yes, I know," Natalie agreed. "If you want, I'll have Bryon call all the boys and let them know we're canceling."

"You might as well," he conceded. "There's no way we can beat this weather."

Natalie stared at the walls desperately, waiting, hoping he would say something else. When he didn't, she said, "No, you're right about that. But your crops are getting a good drink. Have you gotten everything planted?"

"Just about. A few more acres of soybeans is all that's left. I'll have to wait for the field to dry a little before I can finish planting, though."

Natalie could hear soft music in the background, maybe the muted noise of a radio. She could easily imagine the farmhouse he lived in. It had probably been built years ago by his grandparents and the rooms had seen much laughter and tears. It would be a warm, homey place; as full of character as Matt was.

"It was very kind of you to send the roses. Thank you," she said, somewhat embarrassed to mention them.

Her words must have caught him off guard. For a moment he didn't say anything. Then, finally, he said, "I hoped it wouldn't offend you. I—I guess I came on pretty strong the other night. You had every right to be angry at me."

She found herself smiling in spite of everything. "I'm not angry. I know I can be pretty frosty at times. It was probably like waving a red flag at you."

His laughter was warm and husky. "I'm glad I'm forgiven."

Natalie's heart beat faster and stronger. Things she'd never expected to say came to mind.

"To prove it, why don't you come over and share a pot of stew with us? It looks like it's going to be a long, wet evening."

Several anxious moments of silence passed. Natalie felt herself blushing furiously. Obviously, he considered her invitation too forward, or maybe he had plans to be with someone else, in particular, a woman.

"Well, if you've already planned something else," she began.

"No!" his voice boomed back at her. "I don't have other plans. You just took me by surprise, that's all."

To be honest, she'd taken herself by surprise. But now that Natalie had actually invited him, she was glad—very glad.

"Good. By the time you get here, everything will be ready."

"What do I need to bring?"

Natalie's soft lips curved with pleasure. "Just bring yourself. And a hungry stomach."

"Natalie—this makes me very happy. I guess you know that."

Natalie gripped the telephone, feeling his presence beside her, despite the distance between them. His voice did that to her—it had from the very start. She wanted to tell him it made her happy, too, that he was coming. But she couldn't bring herself to go that far. She just wasn't up to it yet.

"See you in a bit," she said, and quickly hung up the phone.

Chapter Six

Thirty minutes later, between intermittent rumbles of thunder, the doorbell rang. Bryon, who had been dogging his mother's steps in the kitchen, took off in a run to answer it.

Matt and Bryon walked through the house toward the kitchen and Natalie listened to the sound of their voices. It seemed so natural to hear them together. Matt's laughter was sprinkled throughout Bryon's excited chatter. The sound was reassuring and comfortable.

"Here he is!" Bryon said as he and Matt entered the dining room.

Natalie turned from the kitchen cabinets to meet Matt's direct gaze. Bryon was standing beside him, a toothy grin on his face.

"So I see." Natalie smiled. "Hello, Matt."

He strolled toward her and Natalie's heart surged. She had no control over her body's reaction to him. How could she possibly have any control when he looked the way he did? Tonight, his hard masculinity was enhanced by the western clothes he wore.

Before he reached her, he took off his broad-brimmed, black hat. His blond-streaked hair lay flat where the band had creased it. With his free hand he pushed his fingers through it, rumpling it sexily across his forehead.

"Hello, Natalie. I hope I'm not late."

Natalie was concentrating so hard on trying to breathe normally that she almost lost her voice. "No—er—you're just right." With a will of their own, her eyes traveled down from his face, across his broad shoulders, then even further, to his waist, where a gold and silver buckle glinted against the tan shirt tucked into his jeans. "I'm glad you could make it," she murmured.

His gaze had never left her face, yet Natalie somehow knew he'd taken in the curve of her legs in her jeans and the peach-colored sweater molded to her breasts.

"I—" He saw that Bryon had turned his attention to the plate of cheese and crackers on the dining table. "I've missed you," he said simply.

Natalie took a shaky breath and lifted her eyes to his. In that instant, she longed to go to him, to kiss him. But Bryon was a mere ten feet away. And even if he weren't, she wasn't sure she could make the first move. She'd always waited for James to set the mood. But with Matt Tanner it wasn't necessary. Romantic, physical things just popped into her head. Had the man caused some chemical change inside her? It certainly felt like it.

"I've missed you, too," she admitted in a low voice.

"Mom, can we eat now? I'm hungry!"

Natalie jerked her eyes away from Matt and saw her son nibbling at a cracker. Her mind came back to the reason Matt was here in the first place. "Yes, why don't you show Matt where he can wash up and I'll finish putting everything on the table."

"Come on, Matt," Bryon urged. "Follow me. I'll show you where you can hang your hat, too."

Matt turned to follow the boy, but not before he'd tossed Natalie a sidelong glance that sent shivers dancing over her skin.

Moments later, Natalie's fingers trembled as she lifted the soup ladle from the granite pot in the middle of the table. Matt passed his bowl to her. She had to concentrate hard so she wouldn't spill all over him.

"I hope you like beef stew," she said. "It's not Bryon's favorite, but it's good when the weather is like this."

"Don't worry," he assured her. "I love stew."

"Well, I don't mind the stew as long as you have corn bread," Bryon chimed in.

Natalie looked at her son's plate. "Sorry, champ, but you're going to have to eat more than corn bread. Stick out your bowl."

Bryon groaned and Matt grinned at him. "Just crumble too many crackers in it," he suggested with a wink. "Then say it's too dry. It always worked with my granny."

Bryon giggled. "Not with Mom. She'll just pour more on it and say eat!"

Laughing, Matt looked over at Natalie as she sat down directly across from him. "Is that your army upbringing showing?"

She smiled in concession. "I suppose. Dad was always a stickler for rules. I've tried not to be like him."

Matt's brows lifted as he caught the faint note of conviction in her voice. He hoped he hadn't hit a nerve with what he'd said. "I was only joking."

She looked at him squarely. "But I'm not. My father didn't know the word 'flexibility' existed."

The look on her face was almost sad. Matt hated seeing it there. He liked when her green eyes were sparkling and smiling at him. "My folks still don't follow the rules. The ones they know about, they've already broken." He laughed.

Bryon looked at him in amazement. "You mean they let you eat just what you wanted?"

Matt's mouth twisted wryly. "Since my parents were hardly ever around, I ate whatever I could scrounge up."

Natalie caught a glimpse of her son's eager expression. Obviously, Bryon was fascinated by this man and his different life-style. Natalie shared his feelings.

"Well, that shouldn't have been too bad," Bryon said. "But where were your folks?"

Matt looked at Natalie as if to ask her how much he should say. "They were traveling, mostly racing horses. My father still trains racehorses."

"Gee, that sounds exciting. I'll bet you had lots of fun doing that."

Matt shook his head. It hadn't been fun. Not when his dad came home with a few too many belts of whiskey in him and his mother yelled and banged things around because he'd left her alone with the kid all day long. She'd never tried to hide the fact she wasn't the maternal type. In his early years, Matt had longed for her affection. But as he'd grown older, that longing disappeared. He'd only been a kid, but even so, he'd known his mother couldn't give the kind of affection a child needed.

"I didn't get to go to the track that much," he told Bryon.

"Do you ever go now?" Bryon asked.

A shadow passed over his face. "No. I'm not that keen on racing."

Natalie studied him as she dipped into the stew. Bryon's questions seem to have dredged up old memories. She wondered what they meant to him.

"The stew is delicious," Matt said, looking at Natalie.

She smiled, amazed at how much she'd wanted to please him. "Thank you. It's nothing fancy."

"You said that you're a farmer." Bryon spoke between mouthfuls of corn bread and milk. "I always thought farmers wore overalls and chewed on a piece of straw. You don't look anything like a farmer."

Matt chuckled, obviously amused by Bryon's frankness, yet Natalie's cheeks flamed beet red.

"Bryon! What a thing to say!" Natalie gasped.

"Aw, Mom," Bryon said. "That's the way they look in my social-studies book."

"Leave the kid alone," Matt said. "He's just being honest." He looked at Bryon, amusement still creasing his handsome face. "So I take it you've never been on a working farm?" he asked.

"No," Bryon said, shaking his head sadly.

Matt looked at Natalie, a question in his blue eyes. She shrugged. "Don't look at me. The closest I've ever been to a farm is the children's zoo or the fields of crops I pass on the way in to Muskogee."

"Well, I think it would be fun to have all those tractors and things," Bryon said, dipping his spoon into his stew. "When can we go see them, Mom? Matt invited us, remember?"

Matt quirked an eyebrow at her and Natalie smiled in response. "Yes, I do remember. And maybe we will— sometime when Matt isn't too busy."

"I won't be busy," he assured her, his blue eyes twinkling. "Especially on Sunday. Why don't you come then?"

Natalie wasn't at all sure about visiting him. Just asking Matt to dinner had been a gigantic step for her. Going to his place seemed like a declaration of how she felt. And if Louise ever found out, God help her!

"Sunday is the pancake breakfast for the little league. Have you forgotten? Or have you begged off from cooking?"

"Cooking?" he repeated in mock horror. "I told you how much cooking I can do. They'll have to put me on dishwashing duty."

Bryon giggled and Natalie laughed softly. The idea of Matt cooking or washing dishes was a strange one. James had done both at times and it had seemed perfectly normal. But she couldn't picture Matt doing anything so domestic. He looked like a man in one of those cigarette ads; a cowboy in a dazzling western landscape. No pots and pans for him.

"I'll do your part of the cooking," she offered.

"Good. I'll repay you by inviting you to my house for dinner. Granny loves to cook for people."

Natalie struggled to keep her jaw from dropping. How could she gracefully bow out of this one. Did she really want to? Inviting him here tonight had told him she enjoyed his company. Agreeing to meet his family would be saying even more. That wasn't wise. She knew there could never be anything serious between them.

"Oh, yeah, Mom! Let's go!"

Bryon's voice broke into her thoughts. The excitement on his face stirred something inside her. He was so fond of Matt. And he needed a male figure in his life right now, even just a friend. She pushed her doubts to the back of her mind.

"We'll see on Sunday if Matt still wants us to visit," she told Bryon.

Bryon could barely contain his excitement over her answer. He wiggled in his seat. Matt threw Natalie a look that made her feel so womanly, heat rose into her cheeks.

"I'll still want you," he assured her, his eyes meeting hers.

They spent the rest of the meal in light conversation about the baseball team and the equipment they should buy once the funds were raised.

Natalie had made a layered devil's food cake the night before. After they'd all had a piece, she suggested that she and Matt take their coffee into the living room where it was more comfortable.

Rain was still falling steadily and it had grown quite dark outside. Natalie pulled the drapes and switched on a couple of lamps. Matt took a seat on one end of the couch.

Natalie sat down two cushions away from him. As she carefully cradled her cup with both hands, Matt crossed his legs at the ankles and looked at her.

Bryon had gone to his room and it seemed terribly quiet. Only the sound of the stereo could be heard, coming from that end of the house.

"I—I suppose this is very dull living compared to what you're used to," she commented.

A wry grin spread slowly across his face. "Not really. Granny and Pa don't act old, but they don't throw too many wild parties, either."

Natalie laughed and shook her head. "No, I don't mean now that you've moved back to Oklahoma. I mean while you were rodeoing. It must have been a fast-paced life.''

He nodded and sipped his coffee. ''It was. Ninety percent of your time is spent traveling. I guess that's why I enjoy being home so much. It's kinda nice to know I'll be waking up in the same bed each morning.''

How many times had he woken up with a woman beside him? Natalie wondered. He was a virile, good-looking guy. There would be plenty of women more than willing to be his partner. Yet she refused to believe that he had been a lady's man. It was very appealing to picture herself by his side, drowsy and contented after a night of making love, however.

She peered at him through lowered lashes, hoping he couldn't tell what she was thinking.

''Bryon and I have lived a very quiet existence since his father died. But I guess you could figure that out by yourself.'' She glanced down at the cup in her hands. Absently, she lifted it to her lips and drank the steaming liquid.

Furtively, he watched her graceful movements. He didn't like to think of her making love to a man, even a man who was gone now. But it was so easy to see himself touching her warm, ivory skin, slowly undressing her and—He forced his thoughts to come to a halt. She'd only asked him to have supper with her. Nothing more than that. He had to remember she wasn't like many of the swinging young girls he'd run into along the way. No, she was infinitely more desirable, because she was everything he wanted in a woman. The dangerous kind, the type of woman who got into your heart and your head.

''How long has your husband been dead?'' he ventured.

Her gaze flashed to his face. Why was she so nervous in his presence? Why couldn't she just relax and treat him like she treated Jerry or some of the other men she knew?

"A little over eight years," she said. "He—he was killed in an automobile accident. The road was icy. He'd been called to the hospital one night—it was an emergency. His car skidded into a diesel."

Her words were devoid of emotion. Had she purposely made them so? He could still feel the smart of her hand on his face from the other night. Matt wanted to think she'd slapped him not because of her husband's memory, but because she'd felt threatened by him as a man.

"So he was a doctor," Matt said thoughtfully.

Natalie nodded. "At Veteran's Hospital. James went through medical school in the army," she explained.

"You said your father was a major. I suppose you met your husband through him?"

Natalie shook her head. "Actually, it was through my brother, Donald. He's a drill sergeant stationed at Fort Bliss, New Mexico. I met James there while I was visiting Donald."

He took a sip of his coffee. "It surprises me that you married a military man."

One of her brows lifted. "Why? It's not surprising at all, really. Military life was all I knew. Military men were the only ones I was ever really around."

"But you weren't exactly keen on the life-style. Or am I wrong in assuming that?"

She shook her head. How had he managed to pick up on her feelings so easily? "You're right. I hated the life-style. But James was a doctor and since he was getting out of the service, it made things a little different."

"And naturally you were in love with him. People tend to forget about occupations and life-styles when that happens," Matt said.

Natalie averted her eyes and forced her shoulders to relax against the cushions. His words caught her by surprise. They made her think back, view things as they really had been. "I wasn't wildly in love with James when I said I'd marry him."

Matt looked at her with confusion. She shrugged, trying to seem casual. "I was eighteen. What does an eighteen-year-old girl know about love?" she asked with a hint of bitterness.

"Precious little, I'd say," he murmured.

She glanced quickly at him and her heart beat sharply, almost painfully in her breast. Natalie knew she'd never been wildly, passionately in love with any man before, including James. But given half a chance, she knew she could be mad about Matthew Tanner. Her feelings were unreasonable, totally without logic. But the feelings were there just the same.

"Oh, well, I grew to love James," she said with a sigh. "He was a quiet, caring man, and I never had to worry about my security."

"Why did you marry him?"

Natalie's green eyes widened. No one, not even her parents had asked her such a question. Yet it seemed so normal for Matt to be asking. And it seemed so right that she was able to answer him truthfully.

"Because I was sure of him, I guess. And I wanted to get away from my father." He narrowed his eyes. She went on, "Don't get me wrong. I love Dad. I just didn't like his rigid ways. And I knew that only someone like James would meet his requirements for husband material."

"You mean you picked your husband to please your father?" he asked, bewildered.

It sounded awful, put like that. But she'd been very young and Major Douglas Winfield had taught his daughter to be like his three sons: to make decisions with her head, not her heart.

"I knew James would make a good husband. He was responsible, dedicated, not given to fits of passion. And mostly he was going to stay in one place."

Matt shook his head and placed his empty coffee cup on the end table. "I didn't know eighteen-year-old girls thought about all those things. I thought they were more romantic."

You would think that, she thought. He had romance and adventure written all over him. The life he'd led epitomized it. She wondered how it felt to let your heart lead you where it would. The idea frightened Natalie; she had always made decisions based on sound logic. "I guess I never was like most young women," she said quietly.

He shifted on the couch so that he was close enough to reach out and touch her forearm. Natalie trembled at the raspy feel of his fingers against her skin.

"Do you know how cold and emotionless you sound?"

She swallowed with great effort. "I guess I am rather emotionless," she said. *But not around you,* she wanted to cry. *Not around you!*

"I don't believe that," he murmured. Just looking at her fiery hair, the little jut of her jawline and the soft, womanly curves of her body filled him with all kinds of emotions. He wanted her to feel that way, too. He wanted to feel her tremble beneath his touch, hear her say she wanted to make love to him.

"You're very young, Matt. You have young ideas."
She tried to reason with him. Yet, as his fingers glided
back and forth across her skin, it was a struggle even to
breathe.

"Damn, Natalie," he said urgently. "That's so ridiculous. You—"

His words suddenly stopped. Bryon was entering the
living room.

Matt pulled his hand away from her. Natalie took a
deep breath and turned her attention to her son. He had
a flat box jammed beneath his arm and from the look on
his face he didn't think it strange at all for Matt to be sitting so close to his mother.

"Mom, can we play Monopoly? There's nothing else
to do since it's raining."

Natalie glanced from Bryon to Matt, trying to decide
if he resented her son's presence. He didn't seem to mind,
but she knew he hadn't come over to play Monopoly.

"Matt may not like Monopoly," she said. She didn't
know if he played any games. As far as that went, she
didn't know how he spent his spare time at all.

Matt grinned at Natalie and scooted to the edge of his
seat. "Just spread the board out on the rug and we'll see
how badly we can beat your mother," he told Bryon.

Bryon laughed and quickly went to work counting out
the paper money. Natalie put her coffee cup aside.

"What do you mean, 'we'?" she asked Matt. "I
thought this game was every man for himself?"

He winked at her. "Us guys have to stick together."

"Hmph," she said, her eyes twinkling. "We'll just see
who's the better investor."

After Bryon had the board set up, they joined him on
the rug and began the game. Bryon, trying his best to
impress Matt, took a long time over his decisions. Nata-

lie played very conservatively, as she always did. However, it was hard to concentrate with Matt stretched out on the rug next to her.

On the other hand, he seemed relaxed and at home. He played extravagantly, just as Natalie had expected him to. Decisions that would have sent her to the poorhouse somehow seemed to end up making him several thousand dollars richer. After about forty minutes, Natalie knew it would be impossible to beat this man.

"Oh, no," Bryon wailed. "Go to jail. I'm going to wind up a convict if I keep on like this."

"At least Matt hasn't taken all your money like he did to me," Natalie said.

Matt chuckled impishly. "You're too much of a tightwad, Natalie. If you'd listened to me and bought those two railroads while you had the chance, you'd be making money."

"Oh, yeah? For your information Mr. Tanner, it would have taken every dollar I had to buy that last railroad I landed on. How can you last without capital to work with?"

He shook his head at her. "You have to be willing to gamble. Nothing ventured, nothing gained, you know."

She grimaced good-naturedly and tossed the dice. "One, two, Park Place. Oh, no!"

"You've had it, Mom," Bryon said. "Matt has a hotel on that. You owe him a mint!"

"No, I don't," Natalie voiced sweetly. "Because I don't have it. Matt will just have to bill me."

"Ha! Bill you! You already owe me several thousand in loans. Hand it over, Natalie."

She looked at him in mock horror. "Matt, I only have two hundred!"

He rubbed his jaw thoughtfully. "That's petty cash. You'll have to give me your house and land on—" He looked at the board, then at her. "Indiana Avenue."

"That's the only house and property I have left," she wailed.

"Sorry, Natalie," he said. He held out his hand, a wide grin on his face.

Bryon began to laugh heartily and Natalie banged her fist against Matt's shoulder. "You greedy scrooge!"

"I'm only getting my due, Natalie," he reasoned between bursts of laughter and trying to dodge Natalie's blows.

"You've got a pile of money! Show a little compassion!"

"That wouldn't be fair, Mom," Bryon exclaimed.

Matt laughed even more at Natalie's indignant expression. "Bryon's right. Face it, Natalie, you're in deep trouble."

Reaching for the title to her property, Natalie stuck her tongue out at both of them. She was just about to slap the piece of paper into Matt's palm when a fourth voice sounded from the doorway leading to the dining room.

"Natalie!"

All three heads turned toward Louise Fuller, who was standing just at the edge of the room with a plastic container clutched in both hands and a face dark with outrage.

"Louise! I—we didn't hear you come in," Natalie said, rising quickly to her feet. She would act naturally—there was no reason not to.

The older woman looked past Natalie's slightly red face to glower at Matt, who stretched easily on the carpet, a pile of money stacked against his midsection.

"Apparently not. I knocked several times," Louise said tartly.

Natalie licked her lips, weighing her options. It was just like Louise to turn up like this. She'd seen Matt's arrival and had conjured up some reason to get a closer look. And boy, was she getting one, Natalie thought, groaning inwardly. The woman's eyes looked capable of burning a hole in him.

"I'm sorry. We were playing a game of Monopoly."

By now Matt had politely risen to his feet. Natalie said, "Louise, this is Matthew Tanner. Matt, this is Louise Fuller, my mother-in-law."

Matt seemed unaffected by Louise's visible disapproval. With a friendly smile, he reached out to shake her hand. "Nice to meet you, Mrs. Fuller."

Louise shook his hand, but failed to reply. Natalie supposed she was too busy ogling him—she was staring openly, a bit rudely, too, as if he were a rare specimen indeed.

"Did you need something, Louise?" Natalie asked.

"Need something?" Louise echoed blankly.

Determined not to let the woman daunt her, she nodded at the tightly clenched container.

"Oh, er, yes," Louise said, finally taking her eyes off Matt. "I—I'm all out of coffee. Harvey wanted me to go to the store, but I told him the weather was too bad. And why should I go to the store when I knew you wouldn't mind?"

Natalie disliked the way she stressed the word 'knew.' Louise knew nothing of the kind, Natalie thought bitterly. *She's probably got enough coffee for three snowy winters hoarded away in that cellar.* But she said aloud, "Of course not. I'll get you some quick so you won't keep Harvey waiting."

She threw Matt a look of apology hoping Louise wouldn't see it. "I'll be back in a minute, guys."

Matt winked at Natalie and Louise stiffened. Natalie's path into the kitchen felt more like the way to the interrogation room.

"Do you need a full can's worth, Louise?" Natalie played along with Louise's excuse as though it were perfectly innocent.

Louise looked at the container and waved her hand as if to bat aside the insignificant question. "Oh, a spoonful or two will be plenty."

Natalie turned her back on her mother-in-law and reached for the coffee canister. Fully aware that Louise would take advantage of having her alone she hastily jerked the lid off.

"Did you invite him over? Again?"

"Yes, I did," Natalie said with a tight grimace.

"I can't believe you, Natalie! Why—he's just a kid!"

Natalie snapped the lid back on the coffee can and whirled around. Her blood pumped through her furiously. It was nearly impossible to keep from screaming at Louise this time.

"He's not a kid, for Pete's sake! He's a grown man, Louise. A farmer, in fact."

Louise clamped her lips shut in a straight line. "Well— he looks awfully young to me! Just how old is he?"

"It doesn't make any difference."

Louise looked at her as though she'd slapped her face. "Doesn't make a difference! My God, Natalie, what's the matter with you?" she hissed, scandalized.

Natalie had been gritting her teeth so tightly, it was a wonder she had any left. "Nothing's the matter," she said. "Age makes no difference where my *friends* are concerned."

Louise folded her arms across her chest, a gesture that always preceded one of her lectures. But Natalie decided this was one lecture that was going to end before it began.

"You know what's going to happen, don't you? Everyone will be talking! They'll say, 'Natalie's making a fool of herself with the new kid in town!'"

Angry words burned Natalie's tongue. Somehow she managed to stifle them. Matt was waiting in the living room and she wasn't going to cause a scene now.

Thrusting the coffee into Louise's hands, she said, "Excuse me, Louise. I'd like to get back to my guest."

Without waiting for a response, she marched around her mother-in-law and out of the kitchen. Let Louise find her own way out—she'd found the way in easily enough.

"Gosh, Mom, you look white," Bryon said as Natalie took her seat beside the Monopoly board.

"Are you okay, Natalie?" Matt asked, his blue eyes solicitous.

Natalie nodded. "I'm okay."

"I'll bet Grandma was asking you a bunch of nosy questions about Matt, wasn't she?"

"Bryon, please!"

The boy ducked his chin. "Well, you know how she is," he mumbled.

Matt's brows arched as he digested this new turn of events. "Don't worry about it, Natalie," he said. "I know it's not personal."

She sighed and met his gaze. He was right. Louise would have objected to Natalie's seeing any man. "Louise and Harvey live next door. That's why James bought this house—so we could live near them."

Matt could read so many things in her regretful expression. He reached over and gave her hand a squeeze. "Come on, forget it. Let's finish the game."

"Louise can be difficult to ignore," Natalie said with a reluctant little smile.

"She got mad at Mom before and hadn't spoken to her in two whole days—'til now."

Matt looked curiously at Bryon. Bryon explained, "Mom bought a new swimsuit. Grandma thinks she's too old to dress that way."

At that moment, Natalie could have wished her son wore a muzzle, but Matt made her forget about Bryon's big mouth. He was laughing uproariously.

"Oh, that's a good one, Bryon!" He turned to Natalie. His blue eyes were soft, mellow and loving. "I can see it's going to be very interesting getting to know you, Nattie."

Chapter Seven

Thirty minutes later, the game ended. Natalie had lost every penny, Bryon finished a respectable second and Matt, of course, was the winning tycoon.

Bryon went to his room to finish his homework, vowing he'd beat Matt the next time, and Natalie invited Matt into the kitchen. She began to brew a fresh pot of coffee.

"I really shouldn't stay much longer," Matt said as he took a seat at the table.

She glanced at her wristwatch. "It's not really that late. Why don't you at least have some cake and coffee before you leave?"

He looked at her pleasantly. "I've never been able to say no to a pretty lady."

Blushing, Natalie cut him a generous slice of cake, then, after a short wait, poured the fresh coffee into two mugs.

When she carried the mugs and the plate of cake to the table, he said, "Where's yours?"

She laughed lightly and patted her hip. "If I ate cake every time I wanted it, I'd never be able to wear that swimsuit."

He chuckled. "Sorry I laughed so hard about that. I just couldn't believe anyone could be that silly."

Natalie smiled ruefully and sipped her coffee. "Louise is—well, I don't know how to describe her. Since I was so young when I married James, she instantly stepped in as a mother figure. And now, even though he's been gone for years, she'd still like to run my life."

"That must be pretty frustrating."

"Frustrating is not the word." Natalie groaned. "Oh, don't get me wrong. She loves me in her own way. If I ever need anything, she's there in a minute. But it—it just gets so stifling, you know?"

Bashfully, she fixed her gaze on his strong, brown hand as he dug into the cake. Matt was so easy to talk to. He'd be so easy to love. Natalie found herself wishing he didn't have to leave tonight—or any other night, ever again. She was treading on dangerous ground, but she couldn't turn back. Each minute she spent with him, each time she looked at him, she knew she was falling fast and hard.

"Yes. I know what you mean." He was looking at her carefully. "Have you ever thought about moving?"

She brushed the red curls back from her forehead. "Oh, yes," she said dismally. "I've thought about it so many times, but I always end up deciding against it. You see James was Louise and Harvey's only child. They live to see Bryon. I wouldn't want them to feel they'd lost him, too."

Matt shook his head. "I didn't mean moving far away—just so you weren't next door to them. You'd be surprised what a difference a mile or two can make."

Natalie shrugged. "They'd think we'd moved to the end of the world. It's a hopeless situation."

"Only if you let it be."

She knew he was right. Things would change only if she made them. It was in her hands. But being a single mother was a big responsibility, and changes were always risky. She looked at Matt. He was so self-assured, so secure in himself. She doubted if anything ever scared him.

"You like Bryon, don't you? And not just because he's my son."

He grinned as he gave her a sidelong glance. "Yes, I like him. He's a great kid. Just by looking at him, I can tell that you're a great mother."

She smiled. "I guess being a mother is the best thing I've done in my life."

Matt looked at her from beneath lowered lashes. She was the sexiest woman he'd ever met. The amazing thing about it was that she didn't even know it. But her looks weren't the only thing that stirred him. There was a wealth of feeling inside her that fit perfectly with him. A strong sense of the value of home and children, love and fidelity. She was a woman he wanted to hold in his arms, to cherish. *Cherish.* The word had never meant so much to him before. He wanted her to have his children, to sleep beside him as they grew older. Could she want that, too?

"It sounds like the rain has stopped. Maybe it's over for good," Natalie said, looking toward the patio doors.

Matt followed her gaze. It was pitch black outside— impossible to see what the weather was doing. Glad for a reason to break his heavy train of thought, Matt stood and walked to the sliding doors.

"I think I'll see if it's clearing," he said.

She rose from her chair and joined him as he pulled the door open and stepped out onto the patio. A cool north wind was blowing. Natalie hugged her arms against her chest as she looked up at the dark sky.

"The stars are hidden, but at least it's not raining," Matt said quietly.

Natalie took a deep breath of the rain-fresh air. "It'll be clear tomorrow. The cold is moving in."

She shivered, ever so slightly. Matt turned toward her. "You're cold," he said. "We'd better go back in."

"I'm not cold," she assured him. "It's only a few goose bumps."

He moved closer, reached out and rubbed his palms over her bare arms. Natalie looked at his face. A heated excitement rushed through her. It was very dark, but there was just enough light coming through the glass doors behind them to illuminate him. The pure masculine lines of his lips were etched by shadow. A bittersweet longing began to ache deep inside her.

She lifted her hands to the hard planes of his stomach, then slid them slowly up the wall of his chest.

"Natalie," he whispered, "beautiful Natalie." He wrapped his arms around her.

Matt pulled her up on her tiptoes as their lips met. He pressed her body firmly against him and her hands came up to stroke the hard flesh of his back. All she could feel was his mouth, that beautiful mouth that smiled at her, spoke to her and kissed her oh so gently.

His touch was as magical and mysterious as the night, full of sensual, erotic promise. Natalie's palms slid up along his spine until they met the nape of his neck. Her fingers linked in a passionate hold against his smooth skin.

Now she tasted hunger on his lips and felt its echo burning deep within her. Thought was impossible—taste and touch overwhelmed her senses. She melted against him.

A husky moan escaped his throat and Natalie shivered with delight as his arms closed around her waist and pulled her even more tightly against him.

"Nattie." He breathed against her cheek. "I've been wanting to hold you, kiss you like this, since we first met." He nuzzled her cheek then parted his lips and traced her earlobe with his tongue.

Drunk with desire, Natalie slid her fingers into his hair and entwined them in the springy curls at the back of his head. "This is crazy, Matt." She sighed. "Really crazy." Yet as she spoke, she scattered hungry little kisses on the musky curve of his throat.

"No, it's not crazy. It's good and right," he murmured. "Can't you feel it?"

Yes! Natalie wanted to cry, but she could barely speak. Her mind was seesawing somewhere between pleasure and panic. "I'm too old for you, Matt. It would never work."

He pulled his head back slightly so that his lips moved against hers as he spoke. "Tell me you don't care for me, that I'm not good enough for you, that you want someone else. But don't tell me that, Nattie!"

"It's true!" she whispered regretfully.

His only reply was the warm, moist touch of his lips on hers. For a moment, the intensity of the kiss swept her away from reality. Her hands left his hair and cupped around the solid strength of his jaw. She held him fast, wanting his mouth never to leave hers, wanting the moment to last forever.

When they were both breathless and dazed, Matt finally tore his mouth away from hers. "I've never wanted any woman the way I want you," he said.

With the kiss broken, sanity slipped back to Natalie in slow, chilling degrees. *The way I want you.* To know he wanted her was thrilling, but it wasn't enough. Not for Natalie. Old-fashioned though it seemed, she needed more before she could give herself completely to him. Matt was young and free—his desires ran on a far different plane.

"I—I'd better get back in," she said, starting to pull away.

He sighed impatiently and lifted her chin with a forefinger so that she looked into his eyes. "You don't believe me, do you?"

For a moment she studied his face—in the darkness it was impossible to read his expression. She doubted she could have, even if they had been standing in broad daylight. She didn't know anything about men like Matt—or much about men in general. The one she had married had been quieter, more passive, and Matt was neither. That frightened Natalie the most. What would it be like to marry someone who could make her lose her head with just the touch of his hand? *Wonderful,* was her immediate response, but it wasn't sensible. She wasn't using her head.

"Yes, I do believe you," she finally whispered.

"Natalie, you're incredible! I tell you something like that and you say you need to go in?"

She let out a deep breath and started to pull herself out of his arms. But Matt wouldn't let her. His fingers tightened around her waist. Mere inches separated their lips.

It was almost impossible to think with temptation so near.

"Look, Matt, we're on different wavelengths. The sooner we face that, the better off we'll be."

"We were on the same wavelength a minute ago," he said huskily.

Natalie blushed bright red. "I—that—that isn't what I meant," she stammered.

His teeth flashed white in the dark. "You say you're too old for me, but right now you're acting very young and foolish."

His words and easygoing attitude rankled her. Jerking herself away from his grasp, she spluttered, "And you're behaving like a—a cocky cowboy!"

Matt's deep laughter halted the steps she had planned to take. How could he laugh at a time like this?

"I *am* a cocky cowboy, Natalie," he said, his rich voice still laced with amusement.

Natalie turned back to him. "How old do you think I am?" She'd folded her arms across her chest.

Rubbing his thumb against his chin, he pretended to mull over her question. "You look about twenty-six."

She let out a sigh of frustration. "Be serious."

His brows arched innocently. "I am being serious."

Her lips compressed to a tight line. "I said how old do you think I am?"

"Okay." His face grew more serious. "Judging from Bryon's age, I'd say you're somewhere around thirty."

"Ha! That just goes to show what a cowboy knows. I'm thirty-three. I was learning to read when you were still in the cradle!"

"So, I caught up with you," he said easily.

Natalie shook her head. "You're hopeless!"

Grinning, he reached out and pulled her back against him. "Come here, you pretty lady. Kiss me again. I want to go home remembering the feel of you, not this foolishness about your age."

In spite of all reason, Natalie couldn't resist him. No man's touch had ever done to her what Matt's was doing now. James's kisses had left her feeling safe and secure, but Matt's kisses made her hot and shaky, set her body clamoring with a need she'd never experienced before. It had to be wrong—anything that could make her feel this high had to be!

"You've—you've got me all mixed up, Matt," she whispered as she broke the kiss.

He smiled, plunging his fingers into the thick, red curls over her forehead and pushing them away from her face. "I'm glad. At least I'm affecting you in some way."

One corner of her mouth lifted. That was an understatement if ever she'd heard one. "You don't know me," she insisted.

"But that's what this is all about—you getting to know me, me getting to know you."

Her heartbeat was erratic as his fingers ran through her hair and came to rest warmly against her throat. "In the end, you may not like what you find," she warned him.

Disbelief curled his lips. "That's not very likely."

"I never have been a gambler, Matt."

"Well, I'm asking you to be one now, Natalie. I know if you give it a chance, we'll have something good together." He leaned down and kissed her softly on the lips, then let her step away from him. "You'd better get back in now. Bryon might be needing you."

He began walking around the vine-covered wall of the patio. She lifted her hand and waved at him. "I'll see you Sunday morning," she called.

He nodded and melted into the shadows. Natalie turned slowly back to the house and stepped inside.

The house seemed too hot after the cool air outside. She pressed her fingers against her lips. They were warm and felt slightly puffy from Matt's kisses. She walked into the living room. Natalie couldn't remember ever feeling so womanly or desirable before. The man had a power over her—a power that both frightened and excited her.

Bryon had gathered up all the Monopoly pieces from the floor and packed them in their box. She looked around for stray glasses and cups—and suddenly spotted Matt's hat hanging on the hall tree.

Slipping it off the holder, she hurried out the front door. He had already started the motor and was backing out toward the street when he spotted her.

He stopped and she went around the front of the truck to the driver's side.

"You forgot your hat," she said as he wound down the window.

"Damn!" he said with humor. "That's the first time that's ever happened. See what you do to me, lady?"

She smiled and handed it to him. "You really know how to feed a woman's ego, don't you?"

With a laugh, he reached out and drew her partially through the open window. "I'm glad I forgot the hat. It gives me another excuse to say goodbye."

Instinctively, Natalie stood on tiptoes and felt again the warm, tantalizing touch of his lips.

"Goodbye," she said softly once the kiss was over.

He put the hat on and an enigmatic little smile creased his face. Natalie watched until he was out of the drive and headed away down the street.

* * *

"That should be enough for now," Leonard said as he looked over Natalie's shoulder at the bubbling pancakes.

Natalie slid the spatula under one fluffy cake and deftly flipped it over. "Are you sure? There's still plenty of batter left."

Leonard looked out over the crowd of people enjoying their breakfast in the school cafeteria. "It's ten-thirty. I think the rush is over. Why don't you finish these up and go take a break. You've been cooking all morning."

Natalie had to admit she was hot and thirsty. Standing over a sizzling grill for more than three hours left her feeling a bit wilted. "Thanks, I'll do that," she told Leonard. "It looks like it's been a success, doesn't it?"

Leonard nodded happily as Natalie stacked the last of the pancakes on a plate and slid it beneath a heat lamp. "I believe we'll have enough for the uniforms and some to spare. We could have used more help here in the kitchen, but at least everyone turned out to eat."

Natalie was a bit disappointed in the Little League regulars. Very few had shown up to help with the preparations this morning. She, Matt, Leonard and two women who were working with the girls' softball teams along with their husbands had done all the work. She'd expected Dan Jenkins to show up and start to throw his weight around, but even he had let them down.

"You know, Leonard, it really burns me that Dan and Rachel didn't show up. He loves to get out on the field and boss the boys around, but I guess he thinks he's too good for kitchen patrol."

Leonard chuckled. "I guess you really aren't in love with him."

Laughing, Natalie untied her apron and tossed it across a wooden work counter. "I guess I made that pretty clear the night of the meeting."

Leonard's brows lifted as he munched on a piece of crisp bacon. "Well, actually, I thought you'd heard about Matt's signing on and wanted to meet him."

Natalie's cheeks burned; she was mortified. Could Leonard possibly know how she felt about Matt? No, she reassured herself, he couldn't. Or at least, not on the night of the meeting—she hadn't even met Matt then. Leonard was only teasing her, but she'd almost given herself away.

Smiling dryly, she said, "I'll just bet you did, Leonard."

He chuckled and glanced down to where Matt and another man were scrubbing the last of the pots and pans. Natalie saw what he was looking at and her curiosity was piqued. "Why did you pick Matt to be my partner?" she asked Leonard.

He smiled broadly. "Matt was a great baseball player. Pitcher in fact. I don't know if he's told you that. Probably not, he never was one to blow his own horn. But he went to college on a baseball scholarship."

The surprise at what he'd said showed on her face. "He didn't tell me anything like that. As a matter of fact, he told Bryon and me that he barely made the roster."

Leonard shook his head. "He would. The guy's won an armload of trophy buckles rodeoing, but you'd never hear him say so. Once in a while, I see him wearing one, but no one here in Fort Gibson or Muskogee actually knows what a success he was."

"If he was that good, why did he quit?" she asked, hoping Leonard wouldn't think she was too interested in the answer.

Leonard shrugged and pushed his large frame away from the warming trays. "He'd always planned to take over his grandparents' farm. Maybe he thought the time had come."

Someone out among the dining tables called to Leonard. With a pensive expression, Natalie watched him walk away. She poured herself a glass of orange juice.

As she walked to the sink, she suddenly realized Leonard hadn't exactly told her why he'd partnered her with Matt. Something made her think he'd skirted the issue deliberately.

Matt grinned as she approached him. "I see you've finally managed to get away from the grill."

She nodded and took a swallow of her juice. "Leonard thinks most of the crowd has come through, thank goodness. How are you guys making out?"

"Finished for the moment," one of the other men said as he laid a metal pot on the drying rack.

"What did Leonard say about the money?" Matt asked.

Natalie brushed damp curls off her forehead. "He thinks we've exceeded our expectations."

"Great," Matt said. "It'll be worth having dishpan hands to see the boys rigged out in flashy new uniforms."

Natalie smiled warmly, peering down at his hands. "Don't worry," she teased. "None of your macho cowboy friends will ever see you like this."

He grinned, fingering the white apron tied around his jeans and yellow polo shirt. "They wouldn't recognize me back here, anyway." He laughed good-naturedly.

Grateful to finally be away from the stove, Natalie took another sip of the orange juice. The pancake breakfast was nearly over. Did Matt remember that he'd invited her and Bryon out to the farm? She'd thought of little else. In spite of the repercussions it might cause between her and Louise, she was looking forward to the visit immensely.

Matt squinted at the thinning crowd. "Nattie, there's a woman out there who must know you or me or both of us. She's been waving in this direction for the last ten seconds."

Natalie turned to look where Matt was pointing. It was Dana and her husband, David, sitting at one of the tables in the back of the room! Without thinking, Natalie grabbed Matt by the hand and led him around the serving line. "Come on, I want you to meet my friends," she told him.

Matt let her pull him between the tables. Several pairs of eyes watched the two of them with interest. No one had ever seen the widowed Mrs. Fuller with a man before—especially not one that looked like Matt Tanner.

"Natalie, did you make the pancakes? They're great!" Dana said as Natalie and Matt reached the table.

"Leonard and I both made them. How are you, David?"

Dana's husband smiled and patted his midsection. "Fine, now that I finally managed to get Dana out of bed and over here to eat."

Laughingly, Dana elbowed her husband and eyed Matt and Natalie. She was really giving Matt the once over, and Natalie could guess what she was thinking.

"Dana, David, this is Matt Tanner. My friend and partner," she announced proudly. "Dana works with me in the women's department," she told Matt. "And this is her husband, David," she said. "Let's see, what do you do, David?" she asked impishly. "Something to do with law enforcement?"

David chuckled dryly and offered his hand to Matt. "I work on the police force in Muskogee."

"Nice to meet you, Matt," Dana said. "Can't you two join us for a moment?"

Natalie looked up at Matt inquiringly. "Think they can manage without us?"

He pulled out a chair and gestured for her to sit. "They'll have to," he said, and gave her a look that was meant only for her.

"Well, are you two planning on winning the league championship this year?" David asked.

Matt shrugged modestly and Natalie laughed. "I don't think Matt believes my team won last year."

"Nattie, I never said that," Matt insisted with a grin. "If you say you won, then you won."

"Natalie's the best coach they have, besides being the only one who's a woman," Dana said, visibly proud of her friend.

With a smile at his wife's enthusiasm, David asked, "How are the boys coming along?"

Natalie pulled her gaze away from Matt's and noticed a smug little smile on Dana's face.

"They're coming along fine. Matt's been working with the pitchers. One of them, Billy Reynolds, is going to be a real hotshot, don't you think, Matt?"

He nodded. "Nattie's done wonders with the infield, too. They're already handling double plays like they've done them for years."

David looked at his wife. "Looks like we're going to have to come and watch the games and see for ourselves."

Dana nodded, her eyes sparkling as she gave Natalie a meaningful smile. "I agree. It looks like things could get very interesting."

Natalie didn't miss the inflection in Dana's voice and decided she'd better get Matt away before her friend said something really embarrassing.

She was just about to suggest they go back to work when David said, "Hey, those are your in-laws, aren't they, Natalie?"

Harvey and Louise! They hadn't said they were planning to come this morning. She would never have expected it, knowing how Louise felt about her coaching baseball—and her association with Matt.

With a hint of dread on her face, she turned to see them carrying a tray loaded with food to the end of a vacant table.

"Yes, that's them," Natalie replied. "I guess they wanted to come for Bryon's sake." More probably Harvey had insisted. There was no way Louise would contribute willingly to the baseball fund. Natalie glanced in Matt's direction. "Maybe we'd better get back to work."

He nodded and pushed his chair back. "You're right. Leonard's going to be yelling if we don't. Come on, we can stop and say hello to your in-laws."

Giving Matt a worried look, she rose to her feet. He knew how Louise was! What was he trying to do, cause a riot? Or was he merely trying to be polite to her family?

As they slipped through the rows of chairs and tables, Matt leaned down and whispered, "I know what you're thinking. But since I intend to be in your life from now on, Louise and her husband might as well get used to me."

She looked up at him and swallowed nervously. "I know you're right, Matt. But she—it—"

He squeezed her hand. "Don't worry, Nattie. Trust me. Okay?"

She nodded, but her legs felt rubbery as the two of them approached the Fullers. *From now on,* he'd said. Was Matt actually thinking in those terms?

"Hello, Mrs. Fuller," Matt said pleasantly. "Are you enjoying the breakfast?"

The gray-haired woman raised her gaze from the plate of pancakes. She wouldn't look directly at Natalie or Matt. Instead, her glare had fastened upon Matt's hand, which rested at Natalie's waist. Natalie was suddenly reminded of Friday night when Louise had interrupted the Monopoly game. She'd insisted that she and Matt were just friends, but that sounded very thin now, even to Natalie. Standing beside Matt now, she knew the way she felt about him was far more than friendly.

"The food is fine."

Louise's tone was cool, but it didn't seem to put Matt off. He smiled and reached out his hand to Harvey.

"I'm Matt Tanner. I help Natalie coach Bryon's team," he said.

Harvey grasped Matt's hand and warmly shook it. "Nice to meet you, Matt. My name's Harvey, but I guess Natalie told you that. Why don't you young people join us and have some of these fine pancakes?"

Louise scowled at her husband. Harvey seemed not to notice. It was rare that he would ignore his wife's wishes. Natalie was surprised to see him do it now.

"We've already eaten, Harvey, but thanks anyway," Natalie told him.

"I think by now they've probably found more work for us, don't you, Nattie?" Matt said.

She nodded with relief. "Yes, we'd better get back to the kitchen. Thank you for coming," she said to Harvey and Louise. "Bryon will be pleased."

"Nice to meet you, Harvey. And nice seeing you again, Louise," Matt said as he and Natalie walked away from the table.

Harvey smiled and nodded. Louise looked down, pretending to be interested in her food. Natalie felt embarrassed by her mother-in-law's attitude, but Matt seemed to take it in stride. When they got back to the kitchen he didn't even mention it.

"I hope we have this mess cleaned up by twelve. I told Granny we'd be out by one o'clock at the latest," he said, glancing at his watch.

He hadn't forgotten the invitation! Natalie felt ridiculously happy. "I thought maybe you'd changed your mind about that," she said.

One side of his mouth lifted wryly. "Not likely, Nattie. I've been looking forward to showing you off to Pa and Granny."

Showing her off! The way he said it, it sounded like he owned her. His words should have bothered her, but the feminine side of her glowed with a warm, appreciated feeling.

Smiling at him, she picked up an apron to tie over her clean lavender blouse and dressy white slacks. "I'm anxious to meet them. Bryon has talked of little else in the last few days."

"Good," Matt said, plunging his hands into the soapy water. He lifted out a fistful of cutlery and began to scrub it clean. He must have felt her eyes on him because he turned and grinned rather sexily. "Well, aren't you going to help me so we can get out of here?"

Her lips tilted with a playful little smile as she sidled up to him in front of the double sink. For the first time since James had died, she felt free. At least fifty pairs of eyes, including those of her in-laws, could see the two of them together. But, for once, she didn't care. Maybe he *was* too young for her. Maybe everyone out there was laughing and calling her foolish. And maybe tomorrow she would regret ever becoming involved with him. But, after so long, she had someone in her life again. Someone who was interested in her as a woman—and as a person.

Matt's arm inadvertently touched hers as he passed her the cutlery to be rinsed. She looked up at him, her lips curving into a purely feminine grin. "I'm glad Leonard paired us together. Not just because of Dan Jenkins, either," she confessed. "We might never have met otherwise."

Her words surprised him but, even more, they made him very happy. Matt's blue eyes softened as he looked at her face. "Something tells me we would have met anyway. Somehow, some way."

Chapter Eight

Is it very far now?" Bryon asked Matt.

They had been driving over a gravel road for the past five minutes. On either side of them, the fields had been disked and plowed into rows that seemed to stretch away to the horizon. It wouldn't be too long before spring arrived. The first tender shoots of green were showing their heads above the reddish earth.

"Not very far now, champ," Matt told him. "Another minute and you'll smell Granny's cooking."

It was a warm, sunny afternoon. The breeze blowing in through the pickup windows lifted and teased Natalie's red curls. The air felt wonderful after she'd been cooped up in the school kitchen all morning. All through the drive out, as she'd sat between Bryon and Matt, she'd thought how even a month ago the idea of going to a man's house would have been preposterous, but now it seemed so right for the three of them to be together. Had she really changed so much? Or had meeting Matt made her see the world in a different way?

She glanced at him and watched the corner of his mouth curl into a grin as he felt her eyes on him. "Hungry?" he asked.

She nodded. "After cooking all those pancakes this morning, I wasn't interested in breakfast."

"Did you plant all this stuff?" Bryon asked. He was sitting on the edge of the seat, his elbow hanging out the window, his dark eyes darting here and there as he tried to take in everything at once.

"Sure did."

"Wow! It must have taken a long time!"

"Not as long as you might think," Matt told the boy. "But it's hard work. You have to discipline yourself to start early and stay late. Think you want to be a farmer?"

Bryon grinned and tilted his head one way and then the other. "I don't know. You'd have to teach me all about it."

Natalie was more than surprised at her son's response. He'd always said he wanted to go into the armed forces like his dad, granddad and uncle. She'd never discouraged him. There were many good points to serving the country that way, but secretly she'd hoped by the time he came of age, his attitude would have changed. She didn't want Bryon to follow in the footsteps of her rigid father. But here was her son talking as if he already planned to have Matt be around to teach him farming.

"I'd be glad to teach you. In fact, it won't be long before you're big enough to drive a tractor."

Bryon's eyes widened. "Gosh! Do you really think so?"

Matt chuckled at the boy's enthusiasm. Natalie's gaze shifted from her son to Matt and back again. Her boy on a tractor? He was only eleven years old, for Pete's sake!

"I don't see why not," Matt told Bryon. "Pa taught me to make rows when I was twelve years old."

Bryon's face lit up with excitement. He did some rapid figuring on his fingers. "I'll be twelve in ten months!"

With a thoughtful look, Matt pushed his hat back. "That'd be just about right. In ten months the spring planting will be starting."

"But I've never been on a tractor," Bryon told him. "How will I be able to drive it?"

"I'll show you," Matt assured him.

"Mom!" Bryon grabbed her knee and shook it back and forth. "Mom, did you hear what Matt's telling me?"

Natalie cast Matt a wry smile then looked at her son. She'd never seen him so animated. "Yes, I heard. But I've also heard tractors are very dangerous."

"They are," Matt spoke up. "But no more than any other machine. You have to handle them with caution and respect."

"I will! Boy, this is going to be great, isn't it, Mom?"

Natalie merely smiled at her son. She couldn't bring herself to echo his enthusiasm. Ten months from now, Matt would have probably forgotten all about them. That much time would be more than enough for him to realize that becoming involved with an older woman wouldn't work. Someone young and new would promptly take her place.

The idea was a somber one. As Matt switched into low gear and pulled slowly over a cattle guard, Natalie did her best to push the thought from her mind.

Country. That was the only way Natalie could describe the house where Matt lived with his grandparents.

It was a white, wood-framed box. The upstairs was the same size as the first floor. On the deep front porch, there were hanging potted plants and heavy metal lawn chairs painted bright yellow.

The small yard surrounding the house was fenced off with barbed wire stretched between cedar posts. Most of the yard and house were shaded by huge elm trees. They were the only trees to be seen and they stood out on the flat farmland.

Off to the left was a small white chicken house with a pen out front. Inside the pen, Rhode Island reds were strutting around and scratching in the bare dirt.

On the south side of the house, the ground sloped, then leveled off to the wide fields beyond. A hardpacked dirt road led to a huge barn made of corrugated aluminum.

The three of them stepped up onto the front porch. Natalie was doing her best to push her curls back in order when the front door opened.

A tall, gray-haired man stood in the doorway. Despite his age Natalie could tell that his build had once been very similar to Matt's—he was tall, lean and strong. He looked very vital and the smile on his face spoke volumes to Natalie. She felt instantly at home.

"Here you are," he said. "Claudie was about to send the law out looking for you if you didn't show up soon. Come in, come in." He held the screen door as Natalie and Bryon entered. Matt followed.

"If you hadn't guessed by now, I'm Amos Tanner," he told them.

"I'm Natalie Fuller," Natalie said, reaching out to shake his hand.

Amos shook Bryon's hand, too. "And I'll bet your name is Bryon."

"Yes, sir," Bryon said politely.

Amos put his long arm around the boy's shoulder. "Well, Bryon, do you like fried chicken?" Bryon nodded. "Why don't you and me go wash so we can beat your mom and Matt to the table. There's only two drumsticks and I think we ought to have 'em, don't you?"

Bryon looked at his mother a bit uncertainly but when Natalie smiled and nodded, he grinned up at Matt's grandfather. "Yeah! I think we should, too!"

Amos laughed and throwing a wink at Natalie, he began to guide Bryon down a narrow hallway off to the right side of the room.

Natalie smiled up at Matt. "I hope your grandfather knows what he's doing."

"Hey, don't worry about Pa," Matt assured her. "He knows all about little boys. He raised me, remember."

"Matt, is that you, son?"

Natalie turned at the sound of a feminine voice. Standing in a doorway at the back of the long room was a short, stocky woman in a dark, printed shirtwaist dress. A blue gingham bib apron was tied over her ample breast. The color almost perfectly matched the blue of her eyes. The woman eyed Natalie with a mixture of warmth and surprise.

"My, my, how pretty you are," she said, then walked into the room. She reached both hands out to Natalie. "My name is Claudie. You're Natalie, right?"

Natalie took the woman's hands and was instantly aware of their smooth, plump warmth. She nodded, a spontaneous smile brightening her face. "It's very nice to meet you, Claudie. I hope you haven't gone to a lot of extra trouble for us."

Claudie patted Natalie's shoulder and began to lead her toward the kitchen, where the aroma of fried chicken and

baking biscuits was strongest. Natalie could feel Matt
following a step behind them.

"Nonsense," Claudie told her. "Sunday wouldn't be
Sunday without fried chicken. Matt'll vouch for that."

The kitchen and the room they had just passed through
were both large, but on first glance Natalie hadn't realized it. Every corner, every nook was filled with pieces of
furniture, many of them covered with doilies and bric-a-
brac. Paintings, photographs, calendars and odd bits of
decorations hung on the walls. The kitchen was even
more cluttered. Pots and pans, bright hot pads and triv-
ets, cooking utensils of all kinds left little room for a few
potted plants. At one end of the room, next to a row of
tall, small-paned windows, sat a large oak table spread
with a white, crocheted tablecloth.

Natalie eyed it admiringly. It would cost a small for-
tune to buy one like it at any antique shop. In fact, she
loved the whole house. It was rustic and homey, a mar-
velous place for working and relaxing.

"Did you bring Bryon, too?" Claudie asked over her
shoulder as she busied herself at the stove. "Amos and I
have been looking forward to meeting him. It's been a
long time since Matt was little. We miss having kids
around."

Matt placed his hand at Natalie's waist and guided her
to the white granite sink at the back of the room. It was
obvious Matt had already told his grandparents about
Bryon. It pleased Natalie that he took such an interest in
her son, but it scared her a bit, too. She'd been telling
herself over and over that her relationship with Matt was
something to enjoy for the moment, but her attitude was
changing.

"Yes, Bryon's here," she told Claudie. "He's gone
with your husband to wash up."

"It's rather informal, but let's wash up here," Matt told her, motioning toward the kitchen sink. "We can't let Pa and Bryon get a jump on us."

Claudie chuckled. "Natalie, you'll find there's nothing formal about us. We just sit back and enjoy ourselves."

Natalie smiled to herself as she dried her hands on a dish towel.

"Matt, go ahead and sit down if you think you can keep out of the food," Claudie said. "Natalie, would you give me a hand here? This pan of biscuits goes on the table and so does the corn."

"Sure, I'll be glad to," Natalie said. She carried the food over to the massive oak table. Matt had already taken a seat. He looked ready to grab a piece of corn on the cob, but Natalie set it down out of his reach.

"Aw, come on, Nattie. I'm starving," Matt pleaded.

"You can wait for the others," she insisted.

"Nobody's waiting for anybody," Amos said as he and Bryon stepped into the kitchen.

"Good," Matt said and reached over to stab his fork into one of the drumsticks.

Bryon rushed toward the table. "Hurry, Amos, he's gonna beat us!"

"Bryon!" Natalie scolded, hardly believing this was her quiet, polite son. "Where are your manners? You know not to run indoors!"

"He's not running, he's just hurrying." Amos chuckled.

"The kid is starved, Natalie," Matt said, siding with Bryon and Amos. "Can't blame him for being hungry."

Bryon beamed from ear to ear at having the two men stick up for him. Natalie was finding it difficult to keep the stern expression on her face.

"This is it," Claudie said as she added a bowl of cole-slaw to the table. "Everybody dig in!"

Everyone took a seat. Natalie sat next to Matt on one side of the table, Claudie and Amos got the end chairs and Bryon was beside Amos and opposite his mother.

Amos said a short prayer, which was followed by the sudden buzz of conversation. Cutlery rattled against glass as everyone passed dishes around the huge table.

Natalie hadn't seen so much food since Christmas Day. Most of the dishes were vegetables prepared in different ways. They all had a wonderful, fresh taste, but Natalie knew it was too early for the gardens to be producing.

"Did you can these vegetables?" she asked Claudie. "Everything tastes so fresh and delicious."

Claudie nodded. "Some of it is canned, some frozen. The garden really put out last year."

Natalie looked at Matt. "Did you grow these things?"

Matt opened his mouth, but Claudie's laughter cut him off. "Matt couldn't keep a vegetable garden. He'd have to use a hoe instead of a tractor."

"Granny!" Matt chided. To Natalie's utter astonishment, he reached over and pinched his grandmother's cheek with rough but warm affection. "Don't be telling Nattie things like that. She'll think I'm lazy!"

Claudie laughed and swatted at his hand with her fork. "You ornery whelp!"

Natalie watched their playful banter with amazement. Her parents had always been so straitlaced, her father insisting on quiet, subdued behavior at the dinner table. And to pinch your own grandmother's cheek! It would be like committing a felony!

"Claudie's afraid of machinery," Amos joined in. "She breaks her back with a hoe 'cause she's afraid to run the garden tiller."

"Amos, that is not true," Claudie insisted. "Besides, hoeing keeps me young."

Matt laughed and winked at Natalie. "She's scared," he said. His grandmother arched a menacing brow at him. "You should see her with the lawn mower. She closes her eyes and grits her teeth when she pulls the start rope."

Across the table, Bryon looked dumbfounded. "Gosh! My grandma wouldn't even know how to run a lawn mower."

Amos laughed heartily, Claudie chuckling along with him.

Bryon spoke the truth, Natalie thought, but she couldn't fault Louise for it. Harvey did all the yard work. There was no reason for Louise to do the things Claudie had to do as a farmer's wife. In that respect, Natalie was just like Louise.

"When you run a farm you have to learn how to do all kinds of things," Claudie told Bryon. "Everybody has to pitch in outside." Claudie looked at Natalie. "Do you work, Natalie?"

She nodded as she swallowed a sip of iced tea. "Yes, I work in a clothing store over in Curt's Mall. It doesn't take any special skill to do what I do."

"Oh, well, I wouldn't say that," Claudie insisted. "I don't know a thing about fashion and that kind of stuff."

"How do you like that chicken, boy?" Amos asked Bryon. "Good, huh?"

Since Bryon's mouth was stuffed full, he merely nodded enthusiastically. Amos grinned and patted him on the head.

"Once we get our stomachs full, what do you say me and you go down to the pond and fish a little?"

Bryon's eyes gleamed with excitement, but, remembering the tractors, he darted a troubled look at Matt.

"Don't worry, I'll have plenty of time to show you the tractors, too," Matt assured the boy.

Natalie stared down at her plate, almost tearful from an overwhelming rush of affection for Matt's grandparents. They had opened their home to her and her son as if they were family. The warmth and love in the room were palpable. What a difference from her own family, Natalie thought.

She wouldn't, couldn't let herself think that Matt had asked other women to share a meal with his family. It was incredible how much she wanted to be special in his life—and that she was letting herself admit it.

The meal was long and everyone got more than his share of delicious food. Just when Natalie thought she couldn't take another bite, Claudie brought out a steaming blackberry cobbler.

Natalie was glad she could still walk as she helped Claudie clear away the dirty dishes.

"Bryon is such a sweet boy," Claudie said, scraping leftovers into air-tight containers. "You must be very proud of him."

"He's my whole life," Natalie said without thinking. Spoken aloud, the words struck her as a bit pathetic. She glanced at the older woman, wondering how she had taken them.

Claudie's face said more than a wealth of words. "Do you think that's good, Natalie?"

"Since my husband, James, died eight years ago I haven't really thought about it. That's just the way it's been."

Claudie smiled as though she understood. "I can see how that would happen, but children grow up and start off on their own lives. When that happens, your life changes.''

A chill rushed over Natalie. Claudie had voiced what Natalie dreaded the most. Bryon was everything to her. What would life be like without him? What purpose or direction would she have?

"You still have Matt,'' Natalie reasoned.

Claudie shrugged. Her brown freckled hands moved efficiently as she dried the iron skillet she'd used to fry the chicken.

"He lives with us for now, but he's got his own life. He'll be wanting a wife and children, and then this old house will just have me and Amos again. But that's the way it should be. We love having him here. But we know he'll go someday.''

In other words, Claudie meant that Natalie needed other things in her life besides Bryon. Was she referring specifically to her grandson? Natalie could have told her that after losing her husband so suddenly and tragically she couldn't easily open her life to another man. For eight years she hadn't been open at all. Meeting Matt had changed that. But she was still afraid.

"Matt is very good with the boys. Bryon adores him,'' Natalie said.

Claudie smiled faintly. "Matt is very fond of Bryon. He's like his grandfather. Amos loves children. It's too bad Matt's father wasn't like him.''

Natalie caught the wistful note in her voice. "Matt says his father lives in New Mexico now. Do you hear from him often?''

Claudie shook her head. "Seldom. Life back here is too slow for Jared. From the time he was a teenager he needed to be near the action, and a farm isn't the place for excitement.''

Natalie smiled and said, "Bryon might disagree with that. He thinks this place is wonderful."

Claudie chuckled. "It takes a special breed to be a farmer. Maybe Bryon is like our Matt. Lord knows Jared hated it. Amos fought with him tooth and nail all the way. In the end, though, it made no difference. Jared's a drifter, an adventurer. He always will be."

Natalie put a pile of dirty plates by Claudie's elbow, then looked at her thoughtfully. "Do you think Matt ever misses his father?"

Claudie shrugged and began to attack the dishes in the sink with a copper scrubber. "No, I wouldn't say he misses him, though I think he regrets he and his father weren't close." She sighed. "How could Matt miss Jared? They hardly knew each other. You see, we've raised Matt since he was very young."

"Yes, I know. He told me."

The woman's eyes lifted from the sink to meet Natalie's gaze. "He did? Well, that's not too surprising. You're the first girl he's ever brought home."

He hadn't brought other women out here! Natalie thought. She was filled with warm pleasure by the news. "You flatter me, Claudie, calling me a girl. I haven't been one of those in a long time."

Claudie snorted. "Nonsense! I'm old, but I'm still a girl at heart. And that's what matters, isn't it? How we feel inside?"

"Yes, I'd like to think so." She could have told Claudie that just being around Matt made her feel very young, completely alive. But it wasn't time for that yet. Perhaps it never would be. Natalie hoped not. Already she felt close to this kind, hard-working woman.

The dishes had been dried and put away when Matt entered the kitchen through the back door. He grinned broadly at Natalie.

"Ready to go fishing?"

Natalie looked at him in astonishment. "Fishing! I don't know anything about fishing," she protested.

"I'm going to teach you. Granny, you want to come, too?"

Claudie shook her head as she folded a dish towel across a rack. "Nope. Too many water moccasins down there for me."

"Snakes!" Natalie gulped. "Matt—I—I don't think I want to go either."

"Granny, hush about the snakes and tell Natalie I'll look out for her," Matt scolded his grandmother. He turned to Natalie. "Bryon's already caught a bass. He wants you to see it."

Natalie groaned in resignation. "Oh, all right. But if—"

"Go on, Natalie," Claudie insisted. "Just 'cause I'm a chicken doesn't mean you have to be."

Matt pulled her out the door before she could make any further protest.

Once she was outside, she had no objections. The late afternoon sun was hazed with a sultry hint of summer. The warmth of it and Matt's hand upon her shoulder were very enjoyable indeed.

It was a fair distance to the pond, but even so, they could hear Bryon's shouts and laughter. Natalie smiled and waved to her son.

"Your grandparents are wonderful to give Bryon so much attention," she told Matt. "He'll never forget this day."

"I hope he has many more like this ahead of him," Matt said. "This doesn't have to be a one-time thing."

She glanced up at him. "He looks up to you, Matt. I hope you know that."

His blue eyes were vivid beneath the brim of his black hat as he looked at her. "He hasn't had that much masculine influence in his life, has he?"

Natalie shook her head, wondering if he'd meant to imply anything about her. "He rarely ever sees my father. And Harvey—well, he's not much of a goer or a doer. That's left me to show Bryon a lot of the things boys do when they're growing up."

His fingers gently squeezed her shoulder. "You've done a good job of parenting, Natalie. I'd be proud to call him mine."

Natalie was so taken aback by his words she nearly lost her footing. By the time she'd recovered they were only a few feet from Amos and Bryon and it was too late to respond. It was just as well, she thought. She didn't know what she would have said, anyway.

"Mom, look at what I caught!"

Bryon pulled a metal fishing basket from the shallow edge of the water and held up a freshly-caught fish.

Amos laughed. "I told him if he catches three more we'll clean them and have Claudie put them in the freezer."

"Maybe Nattie can make it five, if she catches one," Matt said.

Natalie rolled her eyes doubtfully and Bryon said, "Look, Mom! Amos taught me to cast. Watch how easy it is! Think you can do it?"

Natalie watched the fishing line and float sail though the air, then land with a soft plop next to a lily pad.

"I don't know," she said, "I'll try, though."

Matt was already tying a float to one of the rods that was leaning against a fence. When he stood up from his squatting position and handed the rod to her, Natalie had the urge to run away.

"Why don't *you* catch the fifth one?" she said, hedging.

Grinning, he shook his head. "I want *you* to. Look, there's nothing to it." He walked to the edge of the water and Natalie followed him. "Stay on my left so I don't whack you in the head."

She nodded and he began to show her how the reel worked. "The only thing you have to remember is to push the button to release the line and let go when you want it to stop."

"But that's like patting your head and rubbing your stomach at the same time," she argued.

"No, it isn't." He chuckled. "It's not that hard. Just pull your arm back and throw it in the direction you want it to go."

He gave her the rod and reel and Natalie tried to get used to the feel of it in her hand. After she'd found a comfortable hold and had her thumb planted squarely on the dreaded button, Matt told her to cast.

She raised her arm and swung the rod out toward the pond. No line or float sailed through the air as Bryon's had done. She looked around in confusion. Matt said, trying not to chuckle, "You didn't push the button. Try again."

Natalie looked at the rod. The button was still in the position she'd started with. "I told you I couldn't do this!"

"Yes, you can. Try again."

The next time Natalie pushed the button, but it was too early. The line and float landed behind them on the grass.

By now Matt was chuckling outright. Natalie frowned at him. "Stop laughing, Matt Tanner. Just because you beat me at Monopoly doesn't mean—" She shook her head at him, but a smile curved her lips. "Oh, you're mean. You really are mean—"

Before she could finish her sentence he stepped behind her and put his arms around her. Natalie was so taken by surprise that her words stopped. His soft laughter went on, warm in her ears.

"You look damn pretty when you're flustered, you know that?" he said, his lips right next to her ear. Putting his hand over hers on the rod, he pulled it back and up. "Here, let me show you. Just follow my movements."

Natalie allowed her arm to swing free with his. He cast the rod toward the center of the pond and she watched the float fly through the air. She couldn't remember anything about working the reel, not when every nerve in her body was tuned to his touch. Matt reached down and reeled the line in.

"Come on, Mom. You can do it," Bryon said from a few feet away.

Matt stepped away from her. "Try it again," he urged. "Just remember how we did it together."

"Okay, but I think it's hopeless," she warned.

This time Natalie forgot to lift her thumb off the button. Instead of landing in the pond, the float rocketed all the way across to the other side. When it fell into a tall clump of grass, Natalie looked at Matt with such shock that he burst out laughing.

"Fish aren't into sunbathing, Nattie!"

His laughter was infectious. Natalie joined him and laughed so hard that Bryon and Amos eventually moved to the other end of the pond, telling them they were scaring off all the fish.

Natalie didn't care. She was having fun. She was with someone who liked her just as she was, someone who enjoyed the light, simple things in life, someone who made her feel very much alive.

Natalie did finally manage to master the rod and reel. She even caught a fish before Matt and Amos decided to take Bryon up to the barn to see the tractors and farm equipment.

Matt had shown Bryon just about every piece of machinery on the place when Claudie and Amos pulled up beside the barn in an old Ford pickup.

Amos leaned his head out the window and called to the three of them. "We want to show Bryon the cows and my new bull. We'll bring him back later."

Bryon didn't have to be asked twice. Without a backward glance, he left Matt and Natalie. He climbed into the truck, and wedged himself between Claudie and Amos as if he'd known them for years.

"I can't get over the difference in Bryon," Natalie said as the two of them ambled slowly back to the house. "He's usually very quiet. Especially with his grandparents."

"Maybe it's because they're different people," Matt remarked.

"Very different," Natalie agreed. "You've met Louise and Harvey. Well, my parents are pretty much the same as the Fullers, even though they have a different life-style. Mother is very much into social functions, and Dad, he's an army officer through and through."

"Our ways must seem very strange to you," Matt said.

She smiled when he put his arm around her shoulders. "Different, but nice. Very nice. This day has been special for me, Matt. Thank you for asking us."

"Don't thank me," he said softly, his eyes on her face. "Just tell me you came because you wanted to be with me."

"I did come because I wanted to be with you," she admitted huskily.

By now they were inside the fence. Matt pushed her gently against the huge trunk of an elm tree and kissed her. The unexpected touch made her lips part and she moaned softly. The tip of his tongue followed the curve of her lips then, as her arms circled his neck, it thrust boldly between her teeth.

"Nattie." He breathed against her cheek, after tearing his lips from hers. "Whenever I kiss you, touch you, it isn't just for the moment. When I kiss you I want to know that it will always be my right. I want to know that even years from now I'll still be able to reach out and touch you—love you."

Her breath caught with shock then fluttered against the strong column of his neck. "Matt—I—you don't know what you're saying."

He pulled back a few inches and cupped her face in the palms of his hands. "I *do* know what I'm saying. I knew from the moment I met you that I wanted to marry you." He looked deeply into her eyes and Natalie was aware of nothing but the sharp beating of her heart, the feel of his rough skin against her face, the warm taste of his mouth still lingering on her lips. "Tell me you'll marry me, Nattie. Tell me that you want to have my children, that you want me to be Bryon's father. That we'll be together now and forever."

Slowly the fingers that had been clinging to the back of his neck lifted and brushed his tan cheek. "Matt," she whispered. Her voice broke and tears welled in her eyes, spilled onto her cheeks. "Matt, I—I love you. But I can't marry you."

Chapter Nine

Matt's body stiffened against hers and his eyes trained a blue gleam on her troubled face.

"Why?"

She wiped at her tears with futility. "I—because of so many things." She sighed.

"Name one," he demanded.

She took a painful breath. "Our ages."

Matt swore heartily under his breath. "That's no reason," he said angrily. "That's only an excuse."

It was Natalie's turn to be angry. "It isn't an excuse! It's something you need to face. How are you going to feel when I'm forty and you're thirty-five? When I'm fifty and you're forty-five?"

The set of his jaw suddenly softened and the corner of his mouth curved lazily, taunting her. "I'm going to feel like taking you to bed and making love to you until you're too weak to argue with me—just exactly the way I feel now."

His words brought on a slow burn that worked its way up her body until even the roots of her hair tingled. "You're not thinking sensibly," she said feeling shaky.

"I'm thinking like a man. A man who loves you."

"You're not thinking with your head," she shot back at him. "Right now you're young. You'll feel differently when I begin to look old."

"You'll never look old to me."

He was so close that each breath she took pressed her breasts just that much closer to him. She could hardly think or speak. Her whole body was crying out for him to make love to her. All those years and she had never hungered for a man. Now this man was bringing her body, her senses, her feelings back to life. She wanted all of it, the love and emotion, the physical passion, the undiscovered pleasure this man could give her. But she was afraid. So afraid. Didn't he know that? Couldn't he see it?

Her hands dropped from his face. As an unconscious gesture of protection against him, Natalie's fingers curled around his wrist. If his hands moved from her face, if they touched her waist, her hips, her breasts, she would be lost.

"I don't know you, Matt. Not really."

His right thumb moved slowly back and forth across her cheek. "You *do* know me. You know all the things that matter."

"Then maybe I should turn things around," she said. "You don't know me. I've lived for the past eight years without a man in my life. It was very hard at first, but I struggled through it. I've made a life for Bryon and myself. It scares me to think about changing things now, at this point in my life."

He lifted a hand and Natalie closed her eyes as the strong fingers threaded gently through her hair. "Nattie, I know I can't offer you the income or financial security your first husband gave you, but—"

Her eyes flew open. "It isn't the money. My Lord, money has nothing to do with it. It doesn't bother me in the least that you're a farmer!"

He looked at her totally bewildered. "Then what is it? What is it about me that scares you?"

Slowly her fingers released his wrist and slid up the hard, warm muscles of his arms. She wondered if he knew how good he felt to her, how gorgeous the cut of his features was, how just the sound of his voice was enough to make a woman melt for him. He could have his pick, but he wanted her. That was scary enough, but—"Losing you, Matt. Having you, then losing you. That's what I couldn't face."

From the look on his face, Natalie knew her answer had thrown him for a loop. "Losing me?" he repeated blankly. "You mean like James? You're afraid I'll die and leave you?"

Natalie suddenly shivered and her fingers tightened on his arms. "Yes, like that," she whispered hoarsely. "Or maybe you'll just grow tired of living with an older woman and decide you want someone else."

He muttered a curse. "I guess there will always be people who can't separate the word 'cowboy' from the word 'womanizer.' You don't know me, or you'd never think that. Sure, I've known some women in the past. I've even gotten what you might call close to a few. But I never felt anything in my heart for them the way I do for you. I never asked them to marry me, to share my life, to have my children. I wouldn't be asking you now if it wasn't what I wanted for the rest of my life."

He sounded so sincere, so sure of himself. Maybe he would never leave her, but how could she ever forget how uncertain, how fragile life was? She had to make him understand!

"One night my husband was warm beside me in our bed. Thirty minutes later he was dead. I can't face that again. I just can't—not with you. I love you too much."

And she did, she realized. She loved him with her heart, her body, every ounce of her being. Losing James had been traumatic, but losing Matt would destroy her.

He curled his fingers around her shoulders and shook her gently. "There aren't any written guarantees, Nattie. Is that what you want? A slip of paper that says I won't die and leave you, or you won't die and leave me? Are you always going to run and hide from life, remain alone and miserable because you're afraid to take chances? Let me tell you, Nattie, God doesn't give out guarantees. He wants us to live the life he gave us to the fullest, and I intend to take everything he offers me. He's offering us a life together. Are you going to run from it?"

"I—oh, Matt." She moaned in confusion. "I don't know. I just know that I love you and I want you."

He lifted his hands to her face. "Say it again, Natalie. Say you love me again."

"I love you, Matt Tanner," she said, her heart in every word.

With a triumphant sigh, he drew her face up to his. Softly, he kissed her top lip, then the fullness of the lower one. "It's going to be all right, Natalie. Just trust me—love me."

"I do, Matt. I—" She couldn't say anything more. His mouth was making a trail of fire from the corners of her lips, down her throat, across her collarbone and then even further as his fingers undid the buttons of her silk blouse.

The spring breeze was cooling with the setting sun, but Natalie was as warm as noon in July. When his hands closed around her breasts, she leaned back against the tree trunk, her legs threatening to buckle beneath her. Overhead, the young, green leaves danced in her vision, just as the burning need for him danced within her. How could she deny him? How could she ever think of her life without him in it?

When his mouth closed over the peak of her breast, she mindlessly thrust her fingers in the curls covering his head. "Matt." She breathed dazedly. "Your grandparents—Bryon—they'll be coming back—"

His hungry mouth deserted the taut nipple. Its rosy red color matched the just-kissed red on her lips. "Another minute," he said, his husky words muffled as his lips sought the other breast. "Give me one more minute. You're so sweet, so good—"

One more minute turned out to be several more minutes. If the distant sound of a pickup hadn't announced the approach of Claudie and Amos, they might have been embracing for ages before they finally tore apart.

Natalie had been embarrassed when her son and Matt's grandparents joined them in the backyard lawn chairs. There was no doubt in Natalie's mind that her lips were red and swollen from Matt's kisses, her eyes cloudy with unquenched desire.

James had never gotten passionate with her when there was a chance someone else might come around. But then, James had never been passionate at any time unless it was in the darkness of their bedroom. Natalie thought everything she had felt in Matt's embrace was written all over her.

Natalie shook her head to clear the memory of Sunday afternoon from her mind. It was Tuesday, her second day back at work. Usually she was into the swing of things by now. But here it was two o'clock in the afternoon and she was no better off than she had been this morning at eight.

"I didn't know you were back here," Dana said.

Natalie looked up from the little couch that took up most of the space in the employees' lounge where she'd been spending her coffee break. Dana was walking through the door, a soda can in her hand.

"I was just having some coffee," Natalie told her friend.

"Jerry holding down the fort?"

Natalie nodded and took another sip of the coffee. Dana sat down on the opposite end of the couch.

"So what's new with you? We've hardly gotten to talk since the pancake breakfast. I've been wanting to tell you how surprised I was when you introduced Matt. You really threw me, Natalie," she said with a naughty grin.

Natalie sighed and braced herself for the interrogation that was sure to follow. "Why?"

"Why? Are you kidding? You introduce that handsome hunk to me and expect me not to be surprised! When you told me about him before I thought he'd be—er—well—"

Dana floundered, afraid of getting into deeper water, and Natalie smiled ruefully. "Older and more reserved? Gray-haired, a slight paunch at his middle? The kind of man who would always know exactly what he'd be doing from one Saturday to the next?"

"Well, yes," Dana said guardedly, then made a flustered noise. "Oh, you know what I mean, Natalie. It's just that you've always seemed so proper. And Matt looks to be the type who could be very improper," she said with a devilish giggle. "Deliciously improper! I'm proud of you!"

Natalie rose impatiently to her feet and tossed the Styrofoam cup she'd been drinking out of into the wastebasket. She'd been pulled this way and that over Matt's proposal. It had consumed her thoughts to the point where she could think of nothing else. "For what?" Natalie said hopelessly. "Getting myself involved with someone I should have never looked at twice?"

Dana watched Natalie pace around the small, cluttered room, her arms hugging her slim waist.

"Why are you saying that? I think it's wonderful!"

Natalie frowned at her. "Yes, you would. You're twenty-five. Matt would be perfect for you."

Dana grimaced, then took a sip of her soda. "On Sunday, it looked like he was perfect for you."

Natalie lifted one hand and pushed the heavy curls away from her forehead. "Sometimes I really believe he is," she said wistfully.

"Sometimes?" Dana asked, aghast.

Natalie looked at the blond woman and shrugged. "Yes, sometimes," she answered. "The other times I think what a fool I'm making of myself, how I'm going to destroy my whole life if I don't do something."

"Do something?" Dana repeated once again. "What do you mean?"

"Like tell Matt there is no way I can marry him!"

"Marry him! He's asked you to marry him?"

Natalie realized she'd just opened a big can of worms. "Yes," she said in a gentler tone. "He did. But—my

God, Dana, don't you see?'' She pressed her fingertips to her temples. "We're—we're all wrong for each other!''

"You are? I don't see that at all. I think he's perfect for you.''

Natalie's brows rose. "Really? Just a moment ago you admitted that you expected Matt to be older, reserved, gray-headed. Not some young cowboy who looks good enough to pose for a centerfold.''

Dana plopped her can of soda down on the coffee table with a frustrated thud. "I said I expected you to pick a man like that,'' she corrected Natalie. "I didn't say that was the kind of man you needed.''

"So now you think you know what kind of man I need?'' Natalie asked with a tired sigh.

"I've always known,'' Dana answered confidently. "It's just taken you longer to find him than I hoped it would.''

Natalie groaned in disbelief. "Damn it, Dana, what do I think I'm doing? What could possibly make me believe I could hold a man like Matt? He's—I'm not used to— James was—'' She broke off, too embarrassed to go on.

"I know,'' Dana said simply. "James wasn't quite so good-looking and sexy. Not quite so passionate or masculine. And Matt is so strong on these qualities that it's overwhelming you. But all of it will fall into place.'' Dana rose to her feet and walked over to Natalie. "Look, Natalie, there are only two things you should be asking yourself.''

Natalie looked at her. "Two things? I've been asking myself a thousand!''

Dana shook her head. "Natalie, do you love this guy?''

A pain trembled in her breast, then grew. "Yes, I do,'' she whispered.

"And does he love you?"

"He says he does."

Dana looked impatient. "Do you believe him?"

Did she? Yes, she believed him with all her heart. She *had* to believe him. Her feelings, her needs had gone too far for anything else.

"Yes, I believe him."

"Well, then," Dana said with a happy sigh. "That's that."

"It's not that simple," Natalie insisted.

"Why not? Or—" Dana looked thoughtful. "Is Bryon the problem?"

"No—not really. He's crazy about Matt. I think they'd get along fine. In fact, Matt—" she looked at Dana and felt her cheeks go red. "He wants to have children. Can you imagine me pregnant again? At my age?"

"Yes, I can imagine it," Dana answered. "Lots of women your age have children. Don't you think you'd like more children?"

Would she? She thought of how it would be to have Matt's baby growing inside her, her middle swelling with new life. It would be wonderful to have his children, their children, to give Bryon a brother and sister.

She'd thought that part of her life was over, that Bryon would be her only child and even if by some wild happenstance she did marry again, it would be to some older man, someone who'd already lived most of his life. Someone who merely needed a companion. But Matt wanted a friend, a lover, a wife, a mother for his children, everything a woman could be to a man. And deep down, that was just what Natalie wanted, too. Only she was too afraid to admit it.

"Yes—" she began doubtfully. "But Dana, just think. By the time the child starts school I'll probably be getting gray hair!"

"So? Get a bottle of hair dye," she quipped.

"Dana, be sensible! You know how it is, the night feedings, the diapers, the colic, the terrible twos, running them back and forth to kindergarten and school events and—" She rubbed her hand desperately across her forehead. "I don't know if I could do it." Yet even as she said the words, a wonderful sort of excitement began to burgeon in her breast.

Dana waved her arm impatiently. "Then what do you want, Natalie? Some old boring codger who thinks mowing the lawn on Sunday is the big event of the week? Where's the woman inside you?"

Natalie closed her eyes and pressed her fingertips against her eyelids. "She's running scared," she said bleakly.

"I think it's more like she's frozen," Dana muttered.

Natalie opened her eyes and started to speak just as Jerry's head popped around the edge of the door.

"Back to work, girls. There are ladies charging through the aisles out here."

Dana groaned and tossed her unfinished soda into the trash basket. Natalie slipped past Jerry and out the door as she tried to pull herself back together. Tonight was baseball practice. She'd be with Matt again. And right now that was the thought she would hold onto.

It was dark by the time all the boys had left the baseball park and she and Matt had loaded all the equipment into his pickup.

He insisted on driving her and Bryon over to Muskogee for a quick supper. Natalie didn't protest. She wanted to be with him, even if they wouldn't be alone.

"What are you two going to be doing Thursday?" Matt asked as the three of them sat in the fast-food restaurant eating juicy hamburgers and thick milk shakes.

"Nothing, as far as I'm concerned. Bryon is going to a camp-out birthday party for one of his friends," Natalie told him.

He glanced ruefully at Bryon, then over to Natalie. "I thought you might want to go to the rodeo. Lyle, my long-time buddy, will be roping."

Natalie had forgotten it was almost time for Muskogee's annual Azalea Festival. The azalea rodeo was just one of the many events scheduled when Honor Heights Park turned into a blaze of color.

"What about you? Won't you be performing, too?" Bryon asked.

Matt shook his head. "My rodeo days are over. I've even let my sanction card expire. But I'd like to see Lyle and some of my other buddies. What about you, Nattie? Think you might like to go?"

She saw the crestfallen expression on Bryon's face and felt her own spirits sink. "It wouldn't be fair to Bryon. And he can't let his friend down on his birthday."

Matt thoughtfully chewed on a French fry. "We'll compromise. We'll go again on Saturday, too. That way, Bryon will get a turn. How's that?"

"Yeah!" Bryon quickly agreed. "I want to see the rodeo, too. I've never been to one."

"You're kidding," Matt said.

Bryon shook his head emphatically. "No, really." He looked at his mother. "You haven't been to one either, have you, Mom?"

"No, not a live one. We've seen one on TV."

Matt clucked his tongue and reached for his milk shake. "I'm ashamed of you two. Living in Oklahoma, right in the heart of cowboy and Indian territory, and you've never been to a rodeo?"

"We've never had a reason to go to one," Natalie told him.

He grinned at her. "Well, you do now. So we're going."

"Have you forgotten the game on Friday?" she asked.

He looked at her wryly. "How could I forget that? It's our first one and I'm half of the coaching staff."

"So you haven't forgotten."

He looked at her through lowered lashes. "Not a thing," he said in a low voice.

Natalie didn't miss the subtle inflection. She glanced over at Bryon and was glad to see his attention was focused on a group of kids that had just walked into the restaurant.

"I'll be ready to go to the rodeo and the game," she told him. But she couldn't tell him she'd be ready for anything else.

As they finished their meal and Matt joked and talked with Bryon, she watched him almost hungrily and wondered how long it would be before he pushed her for an answer. He wasn't the type of man who would wait for long.

It was almost ten o'clock by the time Natalie and Bryon arrived home. Natalie felt the back of her neck prickle as she opened the front door and stepped into the small alcove. A light was burning in the kitchen. She was certain she hadn't turned it on.

"You'd better go wash and get ready for bed," she told Bryon.

"Do I have to?" he moaned. "I'm not sleepy."

"Just go wash, Bryon," she said under her breath. "We'll talk about the rest when you get that finished."

Satisfied that she'd relented that much, Bryon headed down the hall toward the bedroom. Natalie squared her shoulders and headed to the kitchen.

"Oh, you're home tonight after all?"

"What?" Natalie asked in sudden outrage.

Louise was sitting at the dining table, a crossword puzzle spread out in front of her. Very few of the spaces had been filled in. Natalie angrily wondered how long she'd been in her house.

"I thought maybe that cowboy had talked you into staying over with him."

Natalie couldn't believe her ears. "With Bryon along? Sure, Louise."

Louise's eyes widened at Natalie's unexpected retort. "Hmph. Well, I wouldn't put it past him. And Bryon told me you spent the day out at his house Sunday."

"Yes, we did. And for your information he lives with his grandparents."

Louise snorted again. "Too lazy to work for his own place. That's why. All those cowboys are nothing but freeloaders."

Natalie's fingers curled into tight little fists at her sides. She opened her mouth to speak, then decided there was no use. Even if she told Louise how hard Matt worked to make the farm pay, how much he loved his grandparents, Louise would never understand. People like Louise couldn't understand things like that. "Okay, Louise," she began in a guarded tone. "Would you mind telling me what this is all about? It's late. Bryon and I are going to bed shortly."

Louise picked up the crossword puzzle and folded it with an angry sigh. "I decided that since you're bent on making a fool of yourself over this young kid, I've got to take matters in my own hands and make you see just what you're doing."

"And what am I doing?" Natalie wanted to know.

"Doing? You're making a laughingstock of yourself. Why, just this evening Margrete Simms called and said—"

"Margrete Simms is a big gossip." And so are you, Natalie wanted to add.

"Just the same, she said she saw you kissing someone out in the driveway the other night."

"Just someone?" Natalie hissed sarcastically. "Then maybe she was mistaken and it wasn't Matt. It was one of my other lovers!"

"Natalie!"

Natalie ignored her mother-in-law's outburst. Turning, she walked into the kitchen and shoved her handbag on top of the refrigerator.

"I'm sorry, Louise, but I've had enough of your interference. What goes on between Matt and myself is no concern of yours."

Louise jumped to her feet and stalked across the room to Natalie. "No concern! Bryon is my grandchild. I will not have him disgraced by a mother who's decided she wants to play hussy!"

For a moment Natalie was so angry she was speechless. Finally she gritted out, "You don't know what you're talking about, Louise."

"I know what I see," the older woman burst out. "I have eyes and they see a woman who's letting sex and lust rule her thinking. She sees a nice young body and thinks she can relive her youth, when she should be thinking about her son and the dead husband who worshiped her!''

"Worshiped me!" Natalie cried, feeling something inside her snap. "James directed every step I took! He thought that was love. But what James knew about love was just about enough to fill a thimble!"

Louise sucked in a harsh, disbelieving breath. "How can you speak to me like this, Natalie?"

The pent-up breath drained out of Natalie's lungs. "Because I can finally see, now that I've met another man. My marriage to James was very shallow compared to what marriage can be. And to think I've wasted eight years remembering the past!"

Louise went suddenly still, her eyes angry slits focused on Natalie's face. "What do you mean *wasted*?"

Natalie reached up with both hands and pushed the disheveled curls away from her face. "It means that I'm planning to marry Matt. We're going to give Bryon brothers and sisters. But most of all, we're going to be very happy."

"Marry! You can't—what—"

During Louise's shocked spluttering, Bryon ran into the room and flung his arms around his mother's waist.

"Is it true, Mom? Are you and Matt really going to get married? Is he gonna be my dad?"

Natalie looked down at her son's happy face. The joy in his eyes took away the bitterness of every hateful thing Louise had ever said. "Yes, darling," she said, reaching down and brushing the dark hair out of his eyes. "Do you think you'd like that?"

"Yes! Yes! Yes!"

Louise didn't wait to hear anything else. With short, pounding footsteps she marched out the patio door and slammed it behind her.

"And I'm really going to get a brother, too?"

Natalie smiled down at him. "Maybe even a sister. What do you think?"

"I think I'm so happy I'm gonna bust," he yelled and pulled away from her to do a lopsided cartwheel.

In that moment Natalie realized how much Matt had touched and changed them, how hungry she and Bryon had been for someone to complete the circle of their lives. Tears sprang to her eyes and she wiped at them with the back of her hand.

Bryon noticed the wetness on her cheeks and stopped his dancing around. "What's the matter, Mom? Why are you crying?"

She reached out and hugged him. "Because I love you so much," she answered.

He pulled back his head to look at her. "You love Matt, too, don't you?"

She smiled at him through her tears. "Yes. I love Matt, too."

Chapter Ten

Natalie changed clothes three times before Matt picked her up Thursday evening, and even then she wasn't satisfied with the snug-fitting jeans and white shirt she was wearing. But Matt seemed to think she was dressed just right.

He told her how pretty she looked at least five times before they reached the fairgrounds in Muskogee.

Natalie could hardly take her eyes off him. He was wearing a pin-striped brown and white shirt with pearl snaps and long sleeves. The silver buckle he'd been wearing the night they'd played Monopoly was centered at his lean waist. His brown roping boots looked new and shiny compared to the work boots he wore to baseball practice. He looked very dashing, and Natalie told him so.

"So you're resorting to a little flattery now?" he teased.

She linked her arm through his as they started toward the coliseum where the rodeo was being held. The evening air was hot and muggy and thunderheads dotted out the sky around the sinking sun.

"There's no telling what I might resort to where you're concerned," she said with a coy grin.

His blue eyes sparkled beneath the brim of his black hat and he laughed with a devilish growl as he began to lead her along. "Do you realize this is actually the first time we've been out together—alone?" he said.

She shrugged and smiled. "That's the way it is when you date old widows."

"Funny, Nattie," he said and deliberately squeezed the hand on his arm. "Every guy here tonight is going to be eating his heart out to trade places with me."

"Funny, Matt," she retorted, then wrinkled her nose playfully at him as they dodged and wove through the maze of pickups and horse trailers, horseback riders and people walking. "Maybe one of these days I'll let you see me in my French-cut swimsuit."

He flashed her a wicked grin. "You mean Louise hasn't burned it by now?"

Her brows lifted mockingly. "I'd better check my closet. We haven't spoken for the last two days."

"Oh? What was it this time?" He laughed. "A bikini?"

Natalie opened her mouth, wondering just how much to tell him, when a burly-looking fellow in his mid-thirties jogged up and slammed a broad fist into Matt's shoulder.

"You damn sorry cuss, what are you doing here?"

Matt laughed and shoved his attacker away. "Spectatin', old man. Nothing else."

The man, who had dark hair and a broad face, looked down at Matt's feet, then back up to his face. "No spurs, no lariat rope, no horse tagging along beside you. What a pitiful sight."

Matt grinned and put his arm around Natalie. "I've got something prettier than a horse tagging beside me. Natalie, this is Lyle, my old roping partner. Lyle, this is Natalie."

"Nice to meet you, ma'am," he said and reached out to give her hand a mighty pump.

"Hello, Lyle," Natalie returned shyly.

Lyle slapped Matt on the shoulder, tossed him an impish wink then took off in the same trot he'd arrived in. "Gotta go get my entry paid or they're gonna boot me out of this thing. See ya later."

Matt looked after his friend with a faint grin and a hopeless shake of his head.

"What's the matter?" Natalie asked. "Do you wish you were still doing what he's doing?"

He pulled his eyes down to her face. "Are you kidding? I lived eight years of that step-and-go life."

"Is he married?"

Matt nodded. "Yes. Or at least I think he still is. He's got two girls, twelve and thirteen. They rarely ever see their daddy, and Janie rarely ever sees her husband. It hasn't always been easy for them."

Something inside Natalie tightened as he spoke. She knew what it was like to be alone, to raise a child alone, to long for someone to be there to love her, to help her make the right decisions, to fill the long nights.

"I'm sure it hasn't," she said.

The rodeo was new and exciting to Natalie. As each event started, Matt explained what was happening. He knew all about the cowboys' skills and the use of the animals. She hadn't realized what a dangerous sport rodeoing was until she saw several cowboys thrown to the ground, kicked by flying hooves, slammed against metal gates and charged at by vicious-looking bulls with long, deadly horns. It was incredible to her that men found all this enjoyable.

"I think the male gender has something missing upstairs to want to do this for a living," she told him.

Matt laughed heartily. "Aw, Nattie, this is all fun, just little-boy stuff."

"Little-boy stuff," she repeated dryly. "What about the man they hauled off on the stretcher? That didn't look like fun to me."

"I promise you he'll be back on the road in two days. Just dazed in the head is all."

"I think all you cowboys must be dazed in the head. This is wild and crazy."

To prove her point, the crowd roared and applauded as a blue Brahma bull did his best to hook a horn into a clown who was ducking and dodging behind a brightly painted barrel.

Matt chuckled and shook his head. "It's no more dangerous than race-car driving or something like that."

"But a car doesn't have a brain. These guys are trying to outwit animals that weigh about ten times more than they do and can think for themselves."

A smug grin curved his lips. "Aren't you glad I'm out of the business?"

She reached over and threaded her fingers through his. "I'm glad you're right here beside me," she said.

The look in his eyes made her forget they were in a huge crowd. "You're talking my language now."

* * *

Rain was falling when they left the fairgrounds to go home. Natalie thought of Bryon and the camp out. Their tents would be sopping by morning.

"Would you like to come in for coffee?" she asked Matt when he pulled into her driveway.

"If you hadn't asked, I would have invited myself," he assured her.

They left the truck in a run. She handed Matt the house key and shook the water from her hair while he unlocked the door.

Once inside, Matt reached for her before she could even flip on the light switch.

"Forget the coffee," he said huskily. "All I want is you."

Natalie's heart slammed against her ribs as he pulled her up tightly in his arms. He felt so warm, so strong and solid against her. It was like coming home to put her arms around his neck, to bring her mouth up to his.

"I've missed you, Matt." She breathed against his warm, musky skin.

He swung her up in his arms and carried her over to the couch. The only light in the room was the faint glow of the street lamp filtering through the curtains. But it was enough for Natalie to see the hunger on his face as he laid her back against the cushions and brought his mouth down on hers.

By the time he lifted his head, Natalie's mind was swimming, her breath coming in shallow gasps.

"I don't want to live like this any longer, Natalie. I want to make love to you. I want to wake up beside you every morning, lie down beside you every night. I want us to be together. Have you thought any more about becoming my wife?"

With a sigh she reached up and touched his cheek. "That's all I've thought about."

"And?"

He was already loosening the buttons down the front of her shirt. When his fingers finally found her bare skin it was like an electrical jolt.

"I was going to tell you I needed more time to think about it. That we hadn't known each other long enough to make such a big commitment," she murmured.

"You were going to? You changed your mind?" he asked, his voice slurred as his mouth slid across her naked breast.

Her tongue darted out to moisten her lips. "Louise changed my mind. She started on the warpath about you, told me how worthless you were and what a foolish sex maniac I was being to let you turn my head."

Matt suddenly found her words interesting. He lifted his head to look at her with a quizzical expression. "What did you say to that?"

"I told her I was going to marry you."

For a moment her quietly spoken words slipped past him, then unexpectedly he grabbed her shoulders and shook her with ecstatic joy.

"Natalie, do you really mean it? You're not just teasing me?"

She shook her head and suddenly tears of joy and release were streaming down her face. "No, I'm not teasing. I want to be your wife. I want you to be my husband. All the time Louise was talking, I thought of how Bryon and I had been alone for so long and how finding you had changed all that. So, if you wake up ten years from now and decide I'm too old to keep up with you, don't say I didn't warn you in the beginning."

"Lady, you don't have to warn me about anything. I know what I'm getting. And what I'm getting is what I want."

"Including Bryon?"

"I wouldn't have it any other way. Did you tell him?"

She nodded. "He's crazy about the idea of you being his dad."

Matt's expression was suddenly humble. "I promise I'll always try to live up to his respect, Nattie. And I'll always think of him as my own."

"I couldn't ask for more than that." She sighed with happy content. Sliding her arms around his neck, she leaned forward and kissed him on the mouth. "So, Mr. Tanner, when am I going to become Mrs. Tanner?"

"How about the middle of next week? Is that soon enough?" he said suddenly.

"Next week!" Natalie gasped. "That's like saying tomorrow!"

He grinned lustily. "I would say tomorrow. But we could hardly have a honeymoon while coaching a baseball game."

"But when and how? Where are we going to live?"

"With Pa and Granny for a while, if it's all right with you. But I've already got a property picked out and if you like it, we'll get the carpenters started on it this summer."

"A new house? Matt, you don't have to do that for me."

He drew her close and buried his face in her auburn curls. "I want to do everything for you, Nattie."

She nuzzled her lips against his ear. "You've already done everything for me, Matt." He'd made her love and live again. Her world was brand new because of him. "You don't have to do anything else."

"I've got lots of things planned for you, Nattie. But tonight I just want to hold you. I want to hear you say that you'll marry me again."

She smiled in the darkness as he pulled her tightly against him. "I'll marry you, Matt. For richer or poorer, for better or worse, till death us do part."

It seemed that Natalie's busiest days at work were those when she needed every spare minute she could find. To make matters worse, the Friday traffic was thick as she drove the four miles from Muskogee to Fort Gibson.

Bryon was on his bike in front of the house when Natalie parked the car. "You'd better come help me get things ready," she called to him. "I'd like to get to the field early if we can."

He screeched his bike to a halt beside her and jumped to the ground. "Leonard brought the new uniforms over. They're really neat!"

"Good. Maybe that will boost the team's morale. Has Matt called?"

Bryon shrugged. "I don't know. I've been riding bikes with Jimmy."

"I'll call him in a few minutes. Go put your bike away," she told him as she started toward the house.

In her bedroom she hurriedly tossed off the yellow sundress she'd worn to work and pulled on a pair of blue jeans and a red-and-white-striped short top. After she'd secured the hair away from her face with a pair of white combs, she dialed Matt's number.

There was no answer. Glancing at her wristwatch, she saw it was a quarter to six. He was probably already on his way to the field. By the time she and Bryon had loaded the box of uniforms, the ice chest and refreshments and had driven to the ball field, it was six o'clock.

Matt wasn't anywhere to be seen, but the boys were already there and a big crowd was on hand to watch the game. The opposing team was warming up around the infield. Dan Jenkins was at home plate, knocking grounders. He smiled smugly as Natalie piled her equipment against the backstop.

"Looks like we'll be opposing each other this year," he said.

She nodded. "Looks like it. How's your team coming along?"

"You're going to have to work to beat us," he said with infuriating confidence.

Natalie ignored him and motioned for her team to gather around her. She handed out the uniforms and sent the boys to the dugout to change. When that was done, Matt still hadn't appeared and she felt a faint prickle of unease. What could be keeping him?

"Where's Mr. Tanner?" Casey asked. He'd already strapped on the catcher's orange-colored chest protector. The bright color made his red hair and freckles look tomato red. "It's time for us to warm up. Isn't he coming?"

Once again Natalie glanced anxiously at her wristwatch. "He should be here soon. We'll go ahead and warm up without him."

"But, Mom," Bryon exclaimed with obvious distress, "we can't start without Matt!"

Several of the boys joined in with the same kind of sentiments.

"Darling, I'm sorry. We'll have to start." She looked out over the sea of disappointed faces. "Those of you who have starting positions get ready to take your places in the field. The rest of you can sit in a line over by the dugout."

Bryon angrily swatted the side of his leg with his leather mitt. "You just don't want to wait! If—"

"Bryon! Over by the dugout, now!"

Natalie let out a ragged breath as she watched him trail doggedly after his buddies. If Matt wasn't here soon, they would be terribly let down.

For the next fifteen minutes Natalie knocked grounders and pop flies to the infield and outfield. Every few minutes she looked over her shoulder to search the crowd for Matt's face. He never appeared, but Natalie did spot Louise and Harvey sitting at the far end of the bleachers.

Seeing Harvey there wasn't surprising. He usually attended every game, but Louise's being there with him was quite a shock. Natalie couldn't imagine why the woman would show up tonight. She hated Natalie coaching and despised the idea even more because of Matt.

She was just signaling for the boys to take their positions on the field when they all started to point over her shoulder and shout Matt's name.

With great relief Natalie turned and saw him jogging around the end of the dugout and straight toward her and the boys.

"Matt, thank God you're here! It's time for the game to start!"

His expression was rueful as he glanced from Natalie's anxious face to the group of boys clustering around the two of them.

"I know. I'm late—sorry." He took a deep breath then went on. "It couldn't be helped." A grimace tightened his lips as his blue eyes settled back on Natalie's face. "I don't know how to tell you this—"

"What? Is something wrong?" She could tell from the expression on his face that he was upset. Her heart beat anxiously as she waited for him to answer.

"Yes—something has happened. I can't stay for the game. In fact, I've got to leave town now—tonight. Can you manage without me?"

Upon hearing this news, the boys began groaning loudly with disappointment and tossing out worried questions about the game. For the moment Natalie ignored them and tried to gather her thoughts.

Leave town! What was he talking about? She looked around in confusion. "Well, yes, I can try. But—"

"Look Natalie, I know this is rotten timing, but there's not much I can do about it—"

"Where are you going?" she asked desperately. "What's happened?"

He looked at the boys' earnest faces, then quickly back at Natalie. His eyes pleaded with her to understand. "I can't go into it right now. Just trust me, okay? I've got to go. I'll tell you everything when I get back."

His fingers closed over her shoulder and for a moment she thought he was going to lean down and kiss her, but she supposed he suddenly remembered they had an audience. As he backed away from her and the boys, he gave her a little wave.

She called to him anxiously. "When will you be back?"

He shrugged helplessly. "I don't know. It just depends on—on certain things," he said, then he gave the boys a thumbs-up sign. "Go get 'em, boys. When I get back I want to hear that you played your best." His eyes locked on Natalie. "Goodbye, Nattie. I'll see you as soon as I get back."

"Goodbye," she echoed, not realizing she'd whispered the word.

As she watched him walk away, she wanted to both scream and cry. What could be so important? Why couldn't he have at least told her something?

The boys' anxious voices were coming at her from all directions, forcing her to deal with the problems she faced at the moment.

"It'll be all right, team," she tried to assure them. "We'll just do the best we can without Mr. Tanner. Now those of you on the main team go take your positions, the rest of you know what to do."

Slowly she walked out across the diamond to take her place in the coach's box at third base. Her mind was swirling with questions. Looking over at the bleachers filled with spectators, she knew she would have to put them all aside. She owed it to the boys to give them her full attention. They had a game to play. Later, when it was over, she'd try to make some sense out of Matt's behavior.

When the last out of the game was made, Natalie's team had lost by one point. Dan Jenkins approached her as she stuffed baseballs and aluminum bats into a duffel bag.

"Good game, Natalie," he said. "Too bad your partner couldn't make it. Maybe he would have made the difference. What happened to him?"

I don't know! she wanted to scream. Instead she glanced up at Dan without slackening her pace. "There was an emergency. He couldn't stay for the game."

Dan rocked back on his heels and snorted a short laugh. "Looks like you got hooked up with a good one this season, Natalie. I don't envy you."

She shouldered the bag and deliberately stepped around him. "Excuse me, Dan. I've got to see about my boys."

Bryon was very quiet on the ride back home. His chin on his arm, he sat staring out the window. Not until they entered the house and he and Natalie had lugged the ice chest into the kitchen did he speak.

"Where was Matt going, Mom? Couldn't he have stayed for the game and then left?"

"I don't know," she told him quietly. She was disappointed and confused. Probably just as much as Bryon. But right now she had to be a mother first and a woman second. "Something happened that he had to take care of. And you know that Matt wouldn't have missed the game unless it was something very important."

"Then why didn't he tell us what it was? Matt isn't usually like that."

No, he wasn't usually like that, she silently agreed. She'd fallen in love with a responsible, dependable man. That was why this unexpected behavior worried her greatly.

"I know!" Bryon cried with sudden excitement. "I'm gonna call Claudie and Amos. They'll know what Matt's doing."

He started in a run toward the living room. Natalie just as quickly called, "No, Bryon! Wait a minute."

His young face twisted with confusion as he looked at his mother. "Why? What's wrong with—"

Natalie shook her head as the thought suddenly dawned on her that something might have happened to one of his grandparents. If so, it would be better for Natalie to hear the news first. Bryon had grown so close to Claudie and Amos it would upset him terribly if one of them were ill or injured.

She hurried toward the living room. "I'll call them."

Bryon followed close on his mother's heels. Natalie glanced at her wristwatch as she lifted the telephone receiver. It was getting late but she was going to take the chance that she might get an answer. Natalie didn't think she'd be able to get a wink of sleep if she didn't find out something. Her heart beat in slow, anxious thuds as she waited for the call to go through.

"Hello."

"Claudie, this is Natalie. Is—is everything all right out there? Are you and Amos okay?"

There was only a moment's pause, then Claudie said, "Me and Amos are fine. We're just kind of worried about Matt right now."

The old woman didn't sound exactly like herself and Natalie's grip tightened on the receiver. Before she could ask anything else, Bryon began nudging her shoulder.

"What is it, Mom?" he whispered. "Are they okay?"

Covering the mouthpiece, Natalie glanced up at him. "Yes, just hold on," she told him, then spoke into the telephone. "Matt stopped by the ball field just when the game was about to start, Claudie. He seemed very upset about something. I was just wondering if you knew anything about it?"

She could hear the old woman's sigh on the end of the phone line. "Probably not much more than you, Natalie. All we know is that Jared called. He was in some kind of trouble—only God knows what! Matt's gone to see about him."

The air rushed out of Natalie. "You mean his father?" she asked incredulously. It was the last thing she'd expected to hear.

"I'm afraid so. Amos tried to talk him out of going, but Matt wouldn't hear of it. In spite of everything, Matt—loves his dad."

Claudie's voice sounded thick with tears. Hot moisture stung Natalie's eyes, too. She knew that Matt had always been more like their son than Jared. And knowing the conflict they'd had with Jared over the years, it couldn't be easy for them to hear he was in trouble.

"Where is Jared? What's wrong?" Natalie asked after a moment.

"We don't know," Claudie said in a voice more like her usual self. "That ornery Matt wouldn't tell us a thing!"

"Why?" Natalie gasped.

"Said he didn't want us to worry. And if we didn't know anything we wouldn't have anything to worry about."

"Now that makes a lot of sense," Natalie fumed. "If I didn't love him so much I'd like to choke him."

"I know what you mean," Claudie said. "If he wasn't a grown man now, I'd have a leather strap waiting for him when he got back." She sighed and went on, "Natalie, Jared is so damned thoughtless and crazy. There's no telling what he's been up to and if he gets Matt involved in his trouble I—I just don't know."

Natalie swallowed and did her best to sound confident. "Now, Claudie, Matt is a very level-headed, responsible person. He'll know how to handle things."

"Yes, I know that," Claudie conceded. "I just have to keep telling myself that Jared doesn't have any control over his son anymore. But that's hard to do when Matt ran out of here like he had no choice in the matter."

"Jared is his father. I guess he supposed he didn't have a choice."

"No, I don't suppose so," Claudie said tiredly, then added, "well, Natalie, if I hear from him I'll let you know."

"Thank you, Claudie. Good night."

Bryon was waiting anxiously when she hung up the telephone. Natalie leaned back in the armchair and tiredly thrust her hair away from her face. She was exhausted and worried and frustrated and she prayed that Matt would return home tomorrow.

"What happened, Mom? Aren't you going to tell me?"

She glanced at her son. "Matt's father is having some kind of problem. Matt went to help him."

"Oh. Then I can forgive him for missing our game," he said happily, his face a picture of relief.

"You can?"

"Sure. If Matt was in trouble, I'd want to go help him," he said with certainty.

She smiled softly and reached over and pulled her son's head down to hers. "You love Matt, don't you?"

"Yeah," he said. "And he loves me back."

For a moment Natalie hugged him fiercely. "Yes, he loves you back. And when he gets home again, we three will be a family."

The thought consoled her and she held onto it as tightly as she held Bryon.

Chapter Eleven

Three days later, Natalie stood staring out the living room window. Her hands were jammed in the back pockets of her jeans; a worried frown tugged at her face.

Matt was still gone. Neither she nor his grandparents had had any word from him. Natalie hadn't really expected him to contact Claudie and Amos. Not after he'd purposely avoided telling them where he was going or the kind of trouble his father was in. But she had expected him to contact her. It hurt that he hadn't.

All weekend she had stayed close by the telephone. Today at work, she'd half expected to see him saunter into the store or at least call her there. Her spirits were sinking as quickly as the sun was dropping behind the west side of town.

She kept telling herself that Matt had gone for a good reason. Even though he might be a rake, Jared was his father. She might not always agree with her own father, but if he should need her or call for her she would go to him. She couldn't expect less from Matt. One of the things that had drawn her to him in the first place was his close family ties.

But then she remembered how closely bound James had been to his parents. His deep attachment to them had stifled their marriage in many ways. She certainly hoped Matt wouldn't let his feelings toward Jared go that far.

Family. That was her main worry about this whole thing. She wanted to be Matt's family—she and Bryon. She wanted him to feel responsible for the two of them, too. Maybe that was selfish of her, and maybe Matt's unexpected departure was exposing all her old self-doubts. If this separation had proved anything to Natalie, it had been how empty her life would be without him.

Oh, Matt, where are you? Why haven't I heard from you? She silently asked the questions. She needed to see him, needed his warm embrace to reassure her of his love and their planned future.

The questions were still rattling around in Natalie's head when a voice suddenly caused her raw nerves to jerk.

She whirled around to see Louise standing just inside the living room.

"Natalie? I knocked, but I guess you didn't hear me." She walked a bit farther into the room. "Bryon is watching the baseball game with his grandpa. He said you were alone. I thought it would be a good time for us to talk."

A talk with Louise was the last thing Natalie needed at the moment. But there was no getting around it now. She was going to have to let the woman have her say at some point, or they'd never be able to settle their differences.

"How are you, Louise?"

The woman shrugged dismissively. "I'm fine, Natalie. Not that you would know. I haven't heard from you in days!"

In spite of Louise's pushy, know-it-all attitude, Natalie loved her. She knew Louise looked on her as the daughter she'd never had. But at the moment, as Natalie studied the woman's large, stern features, it was difficult to believe Louise cared about anyone.

"I really didn't think you wanted to hear from me, Louise. Not after our last conversation." She struggled to keep the frustration out of her voice.

Louise grimaced, then crossed the room to take a seat in a stuffed armchair. "I admit that day wasn't a pleasant one."

Her eyes cut pointedly over to Natalie and she knew Louise was telling her to sit. Reluctantly, Natalie pulled her hands out of her pockets and walked over to the sofa.

"I'm sorry you feel that way, Louise. I'd really like you to be happy for me."

Louise sniffed as Natalie sank down into the cushions. "That's what Harvey says. Be happy for you." She closed her eyes and sighed, a bit dramatically. "That's hard to do when I'm afraid you're making a dreadful mistake."

Natalie wondered how much lower her spirits could sink. Right now she felt close to tears.

"Why?"

The woman's brows lifted disdainfully. "I told myself I wouldn't go into all this. But since you asked, I feel obligated to." She looked directly at Natalie. "I just can't help wondering what has happened to the calm, level-headed, sensible woman you used to be. What has this man done to make you turn this way?"

Natalie was still trying to decipher what Louise meant by "this way" when the woman asked accusingly, "Have you told your parents that you plan to remarry?"

Natalie shook her head. Things had been much too hectic and unsettled to phone her parents. "Not yet, but I will."

"And what if they don't go along with the idea?"

Natalie let out an audible sigh. "Louise, I can't live my life to suit everyone else. I have to live it for myself, my needs, my wants and the good of my son."

Louise crossed her legs then tapped the air with the toe of her shoe. "Doesn't that sound a little selfish?"

"A couple of years ago I probably would have said yes, but not now. I've come to realize that even though James is gone and our marriage is gone, I'm still a person, a woman with needs just like any other woman. Is that so wrong?"

Louise's toe abruptly halted its tapping as she thoughtfully eyed her daughter-in-law. "Maybe not. Not if you'd picked the right man."

The right man! Natalie's mind screamed. There would never be a right man in Louise's opinion. "Matt is the right man, Louise. Let's both face it, you want me to remain married to James's memory!"

White-faced, Louise jumped to her feet. "That is simply not true, Natalie!"

"I think it is," Natalie affirmed, then added in a gentler tone, "I know you, Louise. Probably even better than Harvey. And I know how much you loved James. No, you didn't just love James, you worshiped him."

"He was my son!" Louise cried as if that explained everything.

"Yes. He was your son. And I think it's wonderful that you cared so much for him. But the part that's not so wonderful is that you've never accepted his death—you can't let him go. In your eyes I'm still James's wife.''

The air rushed from between Louise's parted lips and she sank weakly into the armchair. "Natalie, that's the cruelest thing you've ever said to me.''

Natalie left her seat and kneeled down on the carpet next to Louise's chair. The woman didn't pull away when Natalie gently touched her hand. "If it sounded cruel, it wasn't meant to. I just want you to see this whole situation as it really is. Matt is a good man. He loves me and Bryon. And he'll make Bryon a wonderful father.''

Louise shot her a doubtful look. "He'll probably try to keep me and Harvey from seeing Bryon.''

Natalie smiled, knowing that Louise had just accepted her marrying Matt, whether she realized it or not. "Nonsense. He'd never want to do that. You'll always be Bryon's grandparents. We'll only be a few miles away. You can see him whenever you want.''

Louise looked uncomfortable and she glanced away from Natalie, saying, "Bryon talks about these Tanner people all the time. He'll forget all about me and Harvey—out there on that farm—with them.''

Natalie's heart suddenly went out to her mother-in-law. She should have realized Louise was afraid of losing Bryon's love and affection, perhaps even Natalie's.

"It's true that Bryon is very fond of Claudie and Amos. But that doesn't mean he'll forget you. I wouldn't let him.''

Louise turned slowly to Natalie and this time there was no mistaking the love on her face. Tears welled in her eyes and she nodded somewhat reluctantly. "No, you wouldn't. I know that. It's just that—this whole thing has me shook up. I . . . want you and Bryon to be happy.''

Natalie smiled brightly and patted Louise's arm. "We will be," she said, then added, "come on, I've got fresh coffee in the kitchen. Let's go have a cup."

Later that night, Natalie sat at her dressing table readying herself for bed when Bryon appeared in the doorway.

He'd just gotten out of the shower and his dark hair was plastered over to one side. She smiled faintly as her glance caught the crooked buttoning of his pajama top.

"Ready for bed, honey?"

He nodded, then walked into the room. "Mom?"

"Yes?" she asked, continuing to rub cream on her face.

"Do you think Matt has decided to stay with his dad?"

The circular motion of her fingers stopped abruptly. She shifted around on the stool so that she could see him instead of his image in the mirror. At this moment he looked so sad and forlorn that Natalie longed to hold him and comfort him as she had when he was a baby.

"No, of course I don't think he's going to stay with his dad," she answered with certainty.

"Then why isn't he back? Why haven't we heard from him?"

She'd been asking herself those same questions all day, but she couldn't let Bryon know it.

"I thought you weren't worried about Matt going to be with his dad?" she questioned. "That's what you said the night of the game."

Bryon ducked his head and mumbled, "I wasn't then. But that was three days ago. I thought he'd be back by now."

"He will be soon," she assured him, then added jokingly, "he's the baseball coach, he can't stay away very long or we'll put him on suspension."

Bryon lifted his head and grinned with quick, sure relief. "That's right! And we got a game in a few days. I know he'll be back home for that!"

Natalie smiled at him. Inside she prayed that Matt would be home by then. If not, Bryon would be devastated, especially now that he knew Matt was going to be his father.

Oh, Matt, she thought, a few minutes later as she climbed into bed. Don't let me and Bryon down. We love you and need you.

She'd tossed and turned for at least an hour when the glow of headlights momentarily swept through her bedroom windows. At first, Natalie thought it was someone merely passing by on the street. But an urgent tapping on the front door pierced the quiet and she knew the vehicle must have pulled into her drive.

Hurriedly she tossed back the covers and pulled on a robe. Her heart was hammering against her ribs with sickening thuds as she stumbled out of the bedroom.

At this late hour she could only think that it might be Claudie or Amos, come to tell her news of Matt. But as she groped her way through the dark living room, her mind flashed back to another night so long ago when she'd answered a knock on the door. She'd found a stern-faced highway patrolman on the step. He'd told her that James had been killed.

No! It wasn't anything like that! God, please let Matt be safe, she prayed.

Her hands were shaking as she pulled back the edge of the drapes. When her eyes caught the silhouette of Matt's tall, lean figure, she sighed with undisguised pleasure.

Excitement had her fingers fumbling with the lock. Finally, she managed to open it and swing the door wide. When she did, Matt was standing there waiting for her.

"Matt! Matt!" It was all she could say as she stumbled forward and into his arms. Her heart was overflowing, pouring out its love for him.

"Is this the way you answer all your night callers?" he asked, burying his face in the sweet fragrance of her hair.

The sound of his gravelly, teasing voice was the most wonderful thing she could imagine. The warmth of his hands could easily be felt through the thin material of the robe. It was like heaven to have him touch her again. "I missed you so, Matt! Where have you been? What happened? Why—"

He leaned down and stopped her questions with his mouth. The hunger in his kiss told her exactly how much he'd missed her. Natalie kissed him back with equal need and for long moments her questions were forgotten. Being in his arms again was too good to spoil with words.

It was Matt who finally broke away, whispering, "We'd better go inside. I think some of your neighbors are still awake."

"I think you're right," she said huskily, glancing over his shoulder to see several lights visible in the neighborhood.

Hand in hand, they entered the house and Natalie switched on a low table lamp. A slow smile spread across her face as she turned and studied Matt in the muted light. He seemed tired and his eyes were bloodshot, but he'd never looked better to her.

"You know, cowboy, you're really something. You tell a girl you want to marry her, then you suddenly leave town."

His grin was both sheepish and cocky. "You mad at me?"

She slanted him a pointed look. "Have other girls kissed you like that when they're mad?"

He chuckled and pulled her against his long length. "Other girls have never kissed me like that period. So come here and show me you can do it again."

The kiss was long and lingering. Once it was over Matt pulled her to the couch before he could give in to the urge to kiss her again.

He took a seat at one end and pulled her down next to him. Natalie snuggled close to him, resting her head against his shoulder. His fingers meshed in the curly thickness of her hair as she looked up into his face.

"Before I tell you anything about what happened—I love you, Nattie."

"You'd better," she said softly and her eyes glowed, studying his handsome features.

His mouth twisted wryly. "You think so, huh?"

She nodded and a low moan of pleasure escaped his throat as he pulled her even tighter against him. With a sigh he said, "I expected you to be at least a little mad at me. I didn't explain anything. But then I didn't have much of a chance. Not with a herd of boys surrounding us. Besides," he added rather ruefully, "if I had told you why I was leaving, you might not have understood."

She thoughtfully watched him. "Why do you think that?" she asked gently.

"Because I went to see Dad."

"I know."

His blue eyes flashed at her. "How? Did Granny and Pa tell you?"

She nodded. "They've been very worried about you. So have I," she added.

"I'm sorry," he said. "I didn't want any of you to worry."

"Then why didn't you call?" she asked. "I've been practically glued to the phone, thinking you'd at least let me know what was going on."

He shook his head. "I know I should have," he said regretfully. "But I just couldn't. I didn't want to explain over the telephone."

"Why?"

He made a rueful sound. "I guess you can figure out why. Hell, I don't even want to go into it *now*. But I know I owe it to you."

"Yes, you do. If I'm going to be your wife—"

"That's just it. You're going to be my wife and I'd like to be able to tell you my dad is a moral, upright man, who takes his responsibilities seriously. I'd like to say I'm proud of him, that I want you to get to know him. Instead—I was afraid to call you because I thought once you learned how my father really is, you'd have second thoughts about becoming a Tanner."

His voice softened to a whisper. Natalie could tell it was costing him to say these things. It didn't have to be that way. "Matt, darling, you're being hard on yourself for no reason at all. I'm marrying you because I love you. What your father does or doesn't do would never affect my pride in you."

He looked into Natalie's eyes and what he saw there told him everything was going to be fine. She loved him, she understood what he'd been going through, and she was the kind of woman who would stand by him no matter what happened. He'd missed her like hell these past days. It had proved to him just what he'd been telling her all along—he couldn't live without her.

Matt reached for Natalie's hand and she clung to it tightly. "Where Dad is concerned, I usually have to forget about pride. You can't know what it means to hear you say that."

She smiled tenderly. "Yes, I do. It means a lot."

His mouth curved into a shadow of a grin. "Yes, a lot," he murmured.

"I take it he was in a mess."

"That's putting it mildly." Matt snorted with disgust. "He was in jail."

Her eyes widened. "Jail! Why? What had—"

"He done?" His features twisted wryly. "He'd been racing a couple of thoroughbreds up at Santa Fe. Once the races were over, the owners left and Dad had the job of pulling the horses back home to Riudoso."

"So, what happened?" she said with a little impatience.

He shifted to face her. "They'd won a first and a second. Since Dad was the trainer, he was feeling pretty high about the whole thing. So he decided to pull over at a bar and do a little celebrating. Needless to say, he celebrated a little too much. He wrecked the truck and trailer and injured both horses."

Natalie gasped. "Oh, no! What about your father, was he hurt?"

Matt shook his head. "Luckily, no, though I don't see how he managed it. God, that pickup looked like an accordion!"

She could imagine how difficult it had been for Matt to see exactly how close his father had come to real tragedy. She wished she could have been there to comfort him. "You found him in jail?"

He nodded grimly. "He couldn't make bail. I had to find a bondsman. The worst part was that the owners of the horses were going to press charges. Both horses were worth several thousand dollars and neither one will be able to race again for at least a year."

"I can see why they'd be angry," Natalie told him. "So how were things when you left?"

He reached up and removed his hat, then slowly raked a hand through his thick blond hair.

"Much better. I had several long talks with the owners. Dad has worked for them as a trainer for years now; they know he's one of the best. It worked to his advantage because, after they'd had time to cool off and think it over, they decided to drop the lawsuit if—if Dad agrees to get help with his drinking problem."

"Did he agree to that?" she asked anxiously.

Matt nodded. "Yes, thank God. But I think it was mostly because he was afraid he'd never be able to train again if he didn't. The people he works for are high up, and they could have made it difficult for him to stay in the racing business."

Natalie let out a relieved breath. "Well, at least he has another chance. And if this cures his drinking problem, it will be worth the trouble."

He gave her a gentle, melting look. "You really do care, don't you?"

"Of course, I care," she answered softly. "I love you. Your problems are mine, too." Her hands slid up his chest to fasten around his neck. "These past few days I was worried that my opinion might not really matter to you," she admitted. "I was afraid you might have decided that Bryon and I weren't so important to you after all."

His expression was the picture of disbelief. "Lord, Natalie! Whatever gave you that idea? You and Bryon are my whole life now. We're going to be a family, us three, and hopefully one or two more. How could you doubt that?''

She shook her head and felt tears forming behind her closed eyelids. The worries and fears of the past three days were draining away, leaving her trembling with relief. "I don't know," she murmured brokenly. "I didn't know where you were or what you were doing. I spent today trying to convince two other people that you really did love me. I guess I just needed you here to convince me of it, too."

"Oh, my darling," he groaned. "Be convinced. I love you—more than anything."

She clung to him tightly, letting the security of his warm body chase away the last of her fears.

Finally, he said, "So tell me, who were these people you had to convince?"

She pulled her head back far enough to look him in the eye. "Louise, for one."

He grimaced. "Well, I should have known. I guess she did her best to talk you out of marrying me?"

Natalie shook her head. "Actually, we had a long talk. I think she's finally accepted the idea."

"Well, that's good news," he murmured.

"Yes, I was glad about it, too," Natalie said.

His eyes had dropped to her parted lips and she knew his thoughts were already drifting. "Bryon was afraid you might want to stay with your dad," she told him.

This seemed to surprise him more than anything she'd said tonight. "Oh, Natalie! I hope you told him that would never happen. I love Dad in spite of the kind of man he is, and I feel compelled to help him when he asks me. But he has his life and I've got mine—you and Bryon are my life."

Her breath was a soft, sweet sigh across his face. "That's all I needed to know."

His mouth came close and covered hers with such completeness that for long minutes she forgot everything but the urgent desire they felt for each other.

"There is one little worry still nagging me," she whispered a few moments later.

"What is that?" he asked, his voice drowsy as he slid his hands along the curve of her warm back. "Surely you're not still worried about the difference in our ages."

She chuckled softly, realizing how senseless that argument had been. When you loved someone, age had nothing to do with it. No amount of time could separate kindred spirits.

"No, nothing like that. I was just wondering how we were going to plan a honeymoon during the baseball season. What with practices during the week and games on the weekends..."

He cocked a brow at her. "Well, we could ask that guy you like so much to fill in for us—what was his name?"

"Dan Jenkins!" she burst out. "No way, Matt Tanner. I'd never turn our boys over to him!"

He chuckled at her alarm, then pulled her against him with a devilish gleam in his eye. "All of a sudden I see our honeymoon will have to be greatly shortened. What do you say? We don't want to waste any time. Let's start on it right now."

Natalie tossed Matt a knowing little grin as she reached over and clicked off the lamp beside them.

It was all the answer he needed.

*   *   *   *   *

COMING NEXT MONTH

#592 JUSTIN—Diana Palmer
Book 2 in the LONG, TALL TEXANS Trilogy!
Rugged cowboy Justin Ballenger was the man of Shelby Jacobs's dreams, but years ago circumstances had ended their engagement, leaving Justin brokenhearted and bitter. Could Shelby convince him she'd never stopped loving him?

#593 SHERLOCK'S HOME—Sharon De Vita
Arrogant detective Mike Ryce wanted to be little T. C. Sherlock's foster father, but welfare agent Wilhelmina Walker thought he was wrong for the job. So why was Mike gaining custody of her heart?

#594 FINISHING TOUCH—Jane Bierce
Clay Dowling's corporation was threatening to destroy Rose Davis's cozy cottage. She had to fight him, but would she lose her heart to his Southern charm before she won the war?

#595 THE LADYBUG LADY—Pamela Toth
From the moment Cassie Culpepper sprayed Jack Hoffman with the garden hose to keep him from killing her ladybugs, she'd captured his attention. Now he wanted the lovely Ladybug Lady to fly—straight to *his* home....

#596 A NIGHT OF PASSION—Lucy Gordon
The greatest joy in Veronica Grant's life had begun with one night of passion in Jordan Cavendish's arms. But she'd kept their child a secret, and now she and her daughter desperately needed Jordan's help....

#597 THE KISS OF A STRANGER—Brittany Young
In the Scottish Highlands, Clarissa Michaels met James Maxwell, the man who had claimed her heart with one kiss. But Clarissa's life was in danger while she stayed in James's ancestral castle. Had destiny brought them together only to tear them apart?

AVAILABLE THIS MONTH: